It's a Dog's Life

A romantic comedy with canine sidekick

by

Dale Mayer

It's a Dog's Life
Dale Mayer
Valley Publishing
Copyright © 2014

ISBN-10: 1927461669
ISBN-13: 9781927461662

DEDICATION

This book is dedicated to my mother. It's the perfect story for her.

Prologue

Wind whistled through the open door of the garage. Moonlight danced across the broken lock. Troy loved it when people took off for holidays and left their houses wide open and inviting – like this. Sure, there'd been a lock on the door, if that's what you'd call it. He hadn't even needed to tinker; his crowbar popped it in seconds.

The owners had been gone exactly three days. Idiots. They'd forgotten to stop the newspaper. He'd be in and out in no time. If they had some good stuff, he'd come back a second time.

Great neighborhood. Rural and small – it worked for him. He'd been working this ten-block square for two months now. The next couple of blocks were a goldmine of opportunity. Easy pickings.

Hadn't these people heard of alarm systems? Not that he couldn't deal with those, too. But tonight's job was a joke. No dog, no alarm, no locks worth a crap. In and out and then on to the next one.

Hard times had struck the small town. Not only were the regular owners of this house absent, but there were many deserted houses all around it. People who couldn't make their payments, couldn't sell their houses, had walked into the bank and handed over the keys. Only the bank couldn't get their money back, because they couldn't sell the places, either. No one came out ahead on those deals – except him. He did some demo work and stripped out what he could. There was always a market for scrap. Tonight, though, he was looking for the good stuff. The easy money stuff.

Cash, collectibles, electronics, jewelry…anything and everything he could carry out and sell fast.

The neighbors had a dog. But it didn't seem to give a damn. If he crossed into its yard then maybe... As it was, he had enough to keep busy for tonight and maybe tomorrow night without going close to it.

There was a tiny one-bedroom bungalow in the next block. The cutie lived there. He didn't know her name, but he'd caught sight of her one night while casing the houses beside hers.

Small and slim, not skinny...she curved where women were meant to curve. She also lived alone. Something he hadn't been able to forget. He was no low life Peeping Tom, but this girl, well...she'd caught his attention something fierce.

Maybe, he'd swing by for a quick look to see if she was home. Who knows, he might get lucky.

Chapter 1

The Lost for Options Animal Center reminded her of a beehive. People and dogs swarmed toward the sprawling building at the front, while another group appeared to be overtaking the neighboring field.

Ninna Bradford pressed a hand to her temple, wishing the pounding would go away. She could handle crowds, just not stampedes. There were animals – everywhere. The place had been calm when she'd been interviewed several weeks ago.

She grew up without pets and didn't even have friends with dogs. She had nothing against them. She liked them well enough. She just had no experience with them. Zip, zilch, nada. Not that she'd told her interviewer that. She could do the job, which was clerical. And this was the only company in six months to offer her a position.

She closed her eyes and stood on the walkway for a few seconds, nervous to go further. *Breathe.*

Her yoga instructor's voice whispered through her mind. *Remember to breathe, Ninna. Take a deep breath...now release. Good.*

Good, my ass. Fat ass, too. Damn her stupid self to hell for that second muffin this morning. She shouldn't have eaten it the first day on her new job. Of course, a bad case of nerves was the reason she'd given in. And she'd had another bad night before that. With the rash of neighbourhood break-ins lately, it was hard to relax enough *to* sleep. She hadn't been able to shake the feeling of being watched. Then again, any excuse for a banana-chocolate chip muffin worked for her.

"Hey, are you all right?"

Spinning around, Ninna smiled sheepishly at the tall redheaded male moving steadily toward her. He was dressed in black jeans and a gray knit shirt that fit his lean frame perfectly. She had trouble focusing on anything but him.

Why was it some men caused no reaction when they walked by, and then some other guys just made her eyes pop open and her mind turn to mush? Pulling herself together, she said, "Yes, I'm fine. Sorry. I didn't mean to stand in the way."

"No problem." He gazed at her curiously. "You looked lost, that's all."

She was, but that wasn't something to share with a stranger, regardless of his stunning green eyes and thick black lashes. Damn, he must be Irish. Stumbling over her words slightly, she explained, "I'm starting a new job here this morning, so I'm dragging my heels a little."

The look in his eye sharpened, then warmed with male appreciation. "Ninna, right?"

She widened her gaze, barely holding back a flush at his blatant appraising look, "Uhm, yes. Do you work here, too?"

He grinned, his face lighting up and his eyes sparkling. "I'm Stuart Macintosh, the resident vet and animal health instructor for the Center. You'll see me coming and going at all hours. Come on. I'll show you around."

"Oh, wow, thank you." Somehow, without really understanding how, she found herself walking up the last couple of stairs to the Center's front door. She shot a glance around her, but the vet opened the door and nudged her through. "There, that wasn't so bad, was it?"

She blinked owlishly, and something in her expression made him laugh. "You'll be fine. Everyone here is very nice."

"Sure they are," she muttered. They would be unless they found out about her *weirdness.* But that was all better now. At least she hoped so. She'd never have tried for this job otherwise. Still applying for a job was a whole different issue than actually starting a new job. How many other people had grown up without being around animals? Any animal. Ever. How would the animals react to her? Would they sense her inexperience?

"Come this way. Trina is here already, and Stacey, my sister, will most likely be in the back. She usually opens the Center and gets people organized. Even so, it's chaos this morning isn't it?"

Ninna barely heard what he said, overwhelmed by the confusion. "I can't imagine that this many people own dogs. Bentley is a small town. Does everyone come here at the same time?"

The waiting area was full. And an ordinary day or not, it was standing room only for both dogs and handlers. This center served as vet clinic, shelter for the lost animals and as an obedience dog training facility. And those were just the services she knew about. The room they'd entered also looked like it was intended as a community center, with a coffee corner…tables and chairs for lounging. And was that a water fountain close to the floor?

Willing to follow his lead, but still a bit bewildered, she followed the vet forward until they'd reached a large group who were talking...or barking.

Good thing she liked animals…at least she hoped she'd like them – if she had a chance to get to know any.

–Damn good thing, actually.

"What?" she asked Stuart, placing a tentative hand on his arm to get his attention. "Sorry, I missed what you just said."

"I didn't say anything." He motioned to the crowd. "It's hard to hear anything right now. Let's get up to the counter."

"Oh, sorry." Confused, Ninna looked around at the people beside her, to see if one of them had spoken to her. No one was even looking in her direction.

Following Stuart deeper into the crowd, she came out the other side at a large counter. It was tight, but she managed to squeeze up beside him. She could see female staff helping customers sign in for obedience classes. The other half of the crowd appeared to be here for the clinic side of the Center.

Stuart caught the first woman's eye. "Hey, Trina, this is our newest employee. She's a little lost."

Dead silence.

Ninna gulped as dozens of faces turned toward her. Putting on a brave smile, she lifted her hand in a small finger wave. "Uhm, hi."

Just like that, the noise resumed, but at a lower level as people returned to their own conversations. A cheerful looking blonde, who Ninna thought was Trina, leaned forward and grinned. "Hey, welcome to the zoo!" Trina's grin was wide and authentic, and Ninna couldn't help but smile back.

"That's definitely my first impression of the place." She laughed. "Where do you want me?"

"I'd say back here, but there's some paperwork for you to fill out and things are a bit nuts right now. Grab a coffee, find a chair and sit down, and let me work through this crowd. It will ease up in..." She glanced over at the clock. "In about ten minutes when class starts."

With that, Trina turned to someone else and answered a question for him.

Dismissed, and with Stuart disappearing down a hallway, Ninna squeezed away from the crowd. She decided against the coffee and managed to find a comfortable chair by the fireplace. Summertime in the Pacific Northwest was either hot or wet, or hot and wet. Either way, she was glad the fireplace wasn't on. Now in winter, that might be a nice touch. Settled and out of the way, she finally breathed easy.

—I wouldn't get too comfortable if I were you.

Frowning, she looked around, sure someone had spoke to her. Only no one was close enough. And that was just wrong – not to mention scary. This certainly wasn't the time for her old problem to reappear.

—You don't listen very well, do you?

"I would if there was anyone to listen to," she muttered. No one was speaking to her, at least no one within ten feet. That meant only one thing, and she was reluctant to admit that – she was hearing voices again. So not what she needed. Trying to keep her words at a whisper, she couldn't resist snapping back at her disembodied speaker, "What is your problem? Go away."

–*Me? I don't have a problem. You're the one that's too stuck up to talk to me.*

The voice was clear and full of attitude. The person should be in her field of vision. Somewhere.

–*I'm right here.*

She shuddered. She couldn't see anyone talking to her. She tugged the neck of her soft blue t-shirt away from her throat as panic settled in.

–*Ease up, will you? You'll figure it out – eventually.*

A heavy *harrumph,* followed by a huge gusting sigh caught her attention, even as she listened to the voice in her head. She searched the large room. Her glance bounced off a nervous-looking dog then came back to another spot as a huge basset hound did a boneless slide down to the wood floor at the far side of the room. When his chest hit the floor, a heavy sigh gusted out of his mouth. From the sounds of it, the poor thing was exhausted.

–*Yeah, you're there.*

Distracted by the voice, she looked around. "Shut up," she hissed, hoping to see a person approaching her. No one was even close. Neither were any animals.

No, no. This was not happening again. She had spent years in therapy because she thought people, and yes, the odd animal talked to her when they weren't. Therapy had worked, finally – after three specialists…and more medications than a pharmacy had a right to offer. She couldn't allow anything to screw up her mind now, or her new job.

—Well, that's good. Because I'm definitely not nothing. I am something. Mosey's the name, by the way.

Ninna closed her eyes and swallowed hard. *Please let there be a short person somewhere playing a joke on me. Please.*

—Oh, quit your whining. You should be happy to talk to me. I'm happy to talk to you. You know there are not many people that can connect with dogs the way you do. What a great place for you to work.

"Oh. That's not right. This is so not the place for me," she whispered under her breath. But she had to make it work. She was desperate.

—Yeah, about that. A little too late to be making that discovery, isn't it? Didn't you just say something about being broke?

"No, I didn't. I thought something about it." This was the first time there was dialogue, not just hearing voices. And that made this scenario even more bizarre. Realizing her voice had risen, she glanced around nervously.

—Bizarre, smishare. You need to get over yourself. My food dish is empty. Isn't filling it one of your new job's duties?

"Oh, no," she whispered under her breath, afraid of what was to come. "Please don't."

—Please don't what?

"Please don't tell me you're a dog?"

A half snuffle sounded beside her. She stole a quick look. A big black Doberman sat staring at her, his pointed ears tilted in her direction.

She slunk deeper into her chair, giving the dog a wary half smile. It was happening all over again. Damn, she needed to call her therapist.

"He's something isn't he?"

Startled, Ninna looked up to see the owner of the Doberman, or at least the leash holder, smiling down at her. Tall, slim and pink. Ninna winced. Surely there was a law against that much pink being hoarded in one spot. The middle-aged woman said, "He's really gentle. He looks dangerous, but he's a kind soul."

Ninna relaxed slightly and laughed. "That's great. I'd hate to meet him alone at night."

"No worries. He sleeps on my double bed, complaining that my husband and I haven't left him enough room."

Wow. That dog was so big she'd never have short-changed his space in the first place. Ninna would have given up her bed and moved to the spare room instead.

As the woman walked away, Ninna surveyed the other animals in the room. Wagging, wiggling, fur-covered canines swarmed the room. Ninna didn't even want to think about trying to figure out *if* one of these dogs was the cause of her derailed imagination.

A small rat-like thing with huge hairy ears, barked at her several times. The sound sent razor blades scraping down her spine. She shuddered. A deep *woof* sounded from the far side of the room. She didn't know the breed, but the furry thing in front of her looked like a teddy bear with a pink bow on its head. She really needed to brush up on her breeds.

Ninna continued to survey the mess of people and dogs until her gaze landed on a ray of sunshine beaming in through the large window and something with a whole lot of skin to fill out sitting beside it – the same huge basset hound she'd seen earlier.

No way. She narrowed her eyes to study the overweight dog before shaking her head. *Nope, impossible.*

–Hey, you found me. Maybe you'll pick this up faster than I expected.

Several dogs walked between them, sniffing the air in her direction.

She studied the new dogs, searching for a sign to confirm which of them might have spoken. With so much confusion and noise, it appeared that no one else noticed anything unusual, so chances were good that the dog wasn't speaking aloud. *Groan.* Of course it wasn't. It couldn't, for God's sake. Animals didn't talk.

She took several deep breaths and tried to relax. She'd heard voices like this before. She'd ignored them back then, and she could ignore this one now.

–Well, ya ain't gonna ignore me. You know how long it's been since I had someone to talk

to? The voice was heavily sarcastic and sounded puffy, as if the speaker were out of breath.

Her stomach knotted and Ninna gulped. Nope. Not happening. She could control this. It was her choice to let that voice in or not. She'd spent years figuring out how to block them out. She'd gotten so good at it, she'd become lax – time had eased the fear, so she'd actually forgotten about the problem, until now.

–Yeah, let me know how that works out for you. I'm so not going away.

Ninna frowned as something odd registered. This time, whoever was speaking had to be reading her mind, and that meant this had to be her imagination.

With that understanding, she broke out in a sunny smile. *Whew.* She could deal with *that.* She'd just make an appointment with her doctor and get her old prescription reactivated and filled. He might need her to see a therapist again, but even that was no trouble. Not considering the options.

–You could just acknowledge that you can talk to dogs. Surely, that would be easier. Stupid people. Always make things more complicated than they have to be.

Dogs? So, I am communicating with a dog? Acknowledge such folly? Hell, no! And why a dog? If she did imagine a talking animal, why not a beautiful wolf, or at the very least, a majestic eagle?

—I'd rather be a bloody horse, but hey, I am what I am. I should have been a Newfoundland dog, but someone screwed up the original orders. So guess what? If I have to deal with it, then so do you.

Gripping the armchair tightly, Ninna opened her eyes and studied the dogs around her – from a little one in a woman's arms to something that was huge and black and white. She thought it was a Great Dane. There was no sign of a Newfoundland dog…if they were the ones that resembled black bears.

—I said I should have been one of those. Geez, don't you listen?

"I don't have to listen to you." Her answer just seemed to slip out on its own.

—Yeah, ya do, unless you're going to drug yourself up or run away again.

Again? How could he know about her history?

—Because you were just talking about it, dumb ass. Maybe you should go and get your

prescriptions filled now. Whatever the pills are.
You're starting to sound like you might need them.

Deep under the disbelief and fear that she truly was on her way to bedlam, irritation and anger stirred. She didn't have to take this, especially if it was her imagination. She deserved respect – no, she demanded it.

–Snort. Let me know when you're looking for some input on that. Not.

"If you're not my imagination and you're not a gorgeous Newfoundland, who and what are you?" There, that should fix the speaker. Thank heavens she was still alone in her corner where no one could hear her. She definitely needed to call her doctor when she got home.

–Go ahead and call him. Get more drugs into your system. Let more doctors into your head. Ignore what's really in there. What do I care? I'm just a dumb basset hound to you. It's not like you're going to listen to me no matter what form I'm in. Your kind never does.

Basset hound? That basset hound from the sun? Had she seen any other one? Really? Okay, that was a bit much. She spun around, looking for the fat one she'd seen earlier. "Okay, smarty pants imagination, I can't see any basset hounds here."

Just then the group of people standing in front of her moved.

The same huge basset hound she'd caught sight of before lay slumped on the floor, soaking up the sunlight, and taking up way too much space in a crowded room like this. With all those wrinkles he looked closer to a skin dog, what is that breed...a shar pei.

—*Oh, aren't you a comedian now? See if I care. Insult me all you want. I know what I am and I know what you are. Someone who refuses to accept what they have. A gift.*

Stunned, she sunk as deep in the chair as she could get, staring in horrified fascination at the boneless mess of patchwork colors. She eyed him carefully. That dog was looking to get stepped on. And was that a food dish sitting beside him? Surely not.

What's wrong with keeping my food bowl close? I want to be on hand when someone fills it. Is that so hard to understand? And you call me stupid. I'm Mosey. You. Are. Psychic.

As she watched, he rolled onto his back, his long ears flapping to the floor on either side of him. Then those loose jowls slopped to the floor as they reformed into a wide grin.

His mouth never moved, but the voice in her head, continued taunting.

–*Boo. I see you.*

Chapter 2

"Hi, Ninna."

Ninna pulled her shocked, disbelieving gaze away from the canine comic on the floor, to see a tall curvy redhead with features similar to Stuart's. The matching bright red hair cinched it. This had to be Stuart's sister. He'd called her Stacey, hadn't he?

Her next statement confirmed it. "Welcome to Lost for Options. I'm Stacey Colbert."

"Uhm, hi, Stacey. Nice to meet you." Flushing with embarrassment, Ninna quickly stood to shake the proffered hand. She couldn't help but feel like plain Jane compared to the statuesque woman in front of her. Ninna had dressed in standard skirt and top for her first day, but Stacey's designer jeans and swanky shirt looked the perfect attire to marry business with chaos.

"Follow me and we'll find an empty office in the back where we can talk." Smiling cheerfully, Stacey carved a path through the crowd.

Ninna cast a last look at the basset hound, only to see one paw drop in a parody of a good-bye wave. A faint sweat broke out across her forehead. She raced to catch up with her guide. They walked through a large set of double doors into a cooler and quieter hallway where the noise level was so much easier on her ears. At the third doorway to the left, Stacey motioned for her to go in.

"I'm going to grab a coffee. Would you like one, too?"

"That would be great, thank you."

"Good, the coffee in here is for the staff. There is coffee out in the main reception room, but sometimes it's impossible to make it through the crowd. You can always count on finding some here." Stacey walked over to the sideboard where there were several coffee makers lined up. She poured out two cups and handed one to Ninna. "There's cream and sugar at the table, if you need them."

Ninna shook her head. "Thanks, but I prefer my caffeine straight."

"Then you should fit in around here. We'd all inject it into our veins if we could." Stacey's smile was wide, genuine and irresistible.

Falling under the friendly spell, Ninna relaxed a little more, realizing she could really be happy here. "Sounds like home already."

"Good. Then let's get you started." Stacey led the way back out to the hallway. "We'll walk around and introduce you to everyone and get you set up at your desk."

"Do I get introduced to all the dogs, too?" Ninna asked.

Stacey laughed. "There're no dogs here on a permanent basis, but you'll get to know the regulars quickly. As for the others, you'll just go crazy if you try to figure them all out at once."

"Really?" Ninna didn't know if she dared to ask, but figured she could get away with it today of all days – as a newbie. "I thought I saw a basset hound out there in the common room?"

"You probably did. We have any number of breeds through here on a daily basis, due to the unique set-up here between the vet clinic, shelter, socializing at the park and the many different classes we offer."

She had to be satisfied with that. Maybe she'd be lucky and never see that dog again.

The rest of the day passed by in a blur. New jobs were deadly.

Perfectly situated, her work was close enough that she could walk home if she chose, something that would save on gas expenses. For her first day, she'd driven to make sure she arrived on time. There was so much to learn, sort through and memorize that she'd used up all the available energy that by day's end she could barely walk at all. The fresh air revived her slightly as she made her way to her car.

The good news was that she'd been so busy for the rest of the day she'd barely thought of her crazy conversation this morning or that baggy basset hound lying in the sunlight.

—Try to forget me, will ya? I don't think so. And who are you calling fat? You're the one who had that second muffin this morning.

Ninna's hand froze, her key remote still pointing at her car door. No. *This can't be happening.* It wasn't right.

—Well, it sure as hell isn't wrong.

"Oh yes, it is," she muttered aloud, hitting the unlock button. Quickly she jumped in and locked the door. Jamming the keys into the ignition, she started the engine. As the purr rippled through the interior of the car, relief shuddered through her. Not another woof or a whimper. She put the car in reverse and backed out of her spot. Turning the wheel, she had to force herself to stay at a sedate pace as she headed out of the parking lot. She couldn't resist one last glance as she drove past.

And wished she hadn't.

Sauntering toward her, across the long covered porch was the same basset hound.

Shit. She'd had enough of him for one day.

But he obviously hadn't.

—You can run, but you can't hide.

She hit the gas and tore down the street.

Ninna parked haphazardly, knowing she shouldn't even have driven home in her current state. That damn taunting voice in her head as she'd exited the lot had finished her. Now she needed a double shot of something. Either that or a mess of Prozac. She fumbled for her house key and finally managed to get the front door open.

She entered quickly, slammed the door closed and locked it. Tossing her purse onto the couch, she raced into the bedroom where she threw herself down on her bed.

It's just my imagination. "It's just my imagination. Oh God, please let it be my imagination."

Her voice grew louder and louder until she was almost screaming with her frustration. Eventually she groaned and ran out of breath.

In the dead silence that followed, her phone rang.

Normal. Mundane. Like it should be.

She pulled her phone out of her pants pocket.

"So, how was first day on the job?" Jane Durant, her best friend, sounded bored as usual. Must be hard to be a daddy's girl with a trust fund – not. Regardless of the difference in their financial realities, the two had met years ago and had been fast friends ever since. "It was fine. Crazy when I got there, but things settled down eventually." Ninna rubbed her sore eyes, wondering how much she dared say.

"Were you nervous? Did you manage to get in the door without having a panic attack?"

Ninna's eyes opened wide. Could that be the answer? The shrinks had warned her that she needed to lower her stress levels. This morning she'd been so scared that something would go wrong – worried she'd get fired – that she had been beyond nervous.

She sat up, grinning. *Yes.* She wasn't going crazy. It had just been a tough day. That's all. Relief at that possibility lightened her heart and eased her mind.

"Hello? Are you there?" Her friend asked.

"Yeah, I'm here. I'm exhausted, though."

"That's to be expected. How about I pick up a pizza and come by? We'll put on a couple of chick flicks and hang out. That will take your mind off the day and you can rest."

Ninna laughed. "What would I do without you?"

A loud snicker came through the phone lines. "You'd replace me with someone else. I have no doubts about that. I'll be there in an hour." Jane hung up.

Ninna didn't want to move – lying on the bed was all the effort she could handle right now – unless it was for a shower. Once the thought of a shower entered her mind, she couldn't shake it. Finally, with only half an hour until Jane's arrival, she dragged herself under the hot water. She'd meant to call her shrink and make an appointment first, but the office would likely have been closed anyway. Maybe it was for the best. If stress *were* the culprit, then her problem should ease on its own by the weekend.

There might even be some old medications lying around – although she knew that wasn't the wisest choice.

Pizza and a movie were perfect for tonight. Pulling on her black stretch yoga pants and top, she headed to the back deck where she moved through a couple of yoga positions and practised her deep breathing. She heard a knock on the door, so walked back inside and opened her front door.

And stopped.

Instead of Jane, it was Stuart, the vet who'd taken her inside the Center this morning.

He looked at her and blinked. "Oh." A big smile broke across his face. "Hi."

"Hi. Were you looking for me?" *She wished.* He was just so...cute. Her sex life had been nonexistent for a long time and he was definitely worth a second look. Besides, he'd been super nice to her this morning and that went a long way to making him desirable, in her books.

He flushed, the color not quite as bright as his hair – but not far off. She watched the wave travel upward with great interest. Poor thing. That had to be hard for a guy to live with.

"From your silence, I gather you didn't know I live here. So let's start again," she said lightly. "Hi, Stuart. What a surprise. What can I help you with?"

He grinned. "Hi, Ninna. No, I didn't know that you lived here. I am glad to see you, though. I'm looking for a little black kitten that's gone missing."

"A black kitten?" Mystified, Ninna took a quick look around on her porch. "I just got home, but I haven't seen any animals. Is it yours?"

"Sort of. He'd been dumped at the Center. He's a runt, a little sickly and didn't seem to do well there, so I thought maybe a different atmosphere would help him out." He shrugged. "Apparently that helped him out a little too much. He's taken off."

Ninna finally realized this cute vet must be one of her neighbours. How sad that she hadn't known that before. "If I do see him, which house is yours, so I can return him?" She looked at the two sides of the street. There was her house, old, small, parked in between several aged and other equally uninspiring houses. Not that those on her block were deserted or unloved, she knew. The owners on one side had lost their jobs and told her they were living on their tiny investments.

And then there was the other side, where a subdivision of large modern houses began. The contrast wasn't so much a monetary difference but one of the old versus the new.

"I'm in that one, with the stone wall out front." He pointed to one almost directly across the street from hers. One of the biggest. She shook her head. He must have a huge family if he needed a house that size. She wondered how long he'd lived there. She'd never noticed him in the neighborhood before. And she would have remembered good-looking Stuart. Not that she spent much time out front. Her backyard was much nicer.

"Okay – if I see him, I'll bring him over to you."

He smiled. "Thanks, I'd appreciate that." He turned and headed toward his house.

Ninna stood on the porch and watched him walk across the road and down the sidewalk. Jane pulled up when he'd almost reached his driveway. Ninna couldn't tear her eyes away from him. She heard him whistle and heard the barking. Next thing she knew several dogs rushed forward to greet him at the yard gate.

Dragging up the rear was the basset hound. He tossed her an open-mouthed grin before following the other dogs inside the house.

***

"So what put that sour lemon look on your face? And here I come bearing gifts. It's pepperoni with ham and mushrooms, your favourite." Tossing her hair, Jane brushed past her with her oversized box. "I got a family size. No comments, please. A girl has to do what a girl has to do."

Ninna turned her attention to her best friend's voluptuous curves. "I hope you're planning on sharing that thing."

"Nope. Go get your own." The laughter in her voice reassured Ninna that she wouldn't have to order for herself. With Jane, one never knew though. That girl could seriously eat.

As soon as she'd closed the front door, Jane spun on her. "Who was that divine looking man? I love his hair. I didn't even know you were on speaking terms with an eligible male. Spill."

"Hey, I'm not a recluse. I know some guys."
Ninna grabbed the pizza box from Jane's arms and
headed to the kitchen. By the time she had the box
open, Jane had already pulled down two plates
and was reaching for the biggest piece.

"Yeah, old fat farts you've known forever."
Jane smirked around the string of hot cheese
dripping from her mouth.

It was a little hard to argue with what Jane
said, since most of the men Ninna knew were her
dad's old friends.

Jane wouldn't let it go. "So…who is he?
Details, please."

Rolling her eyes at her friend's insistence,
Ninna finished swallowing her bite before
answering. "He's one of the vets from the Center.
I met him this morning." With a sheepish grin, she
explained their initial meeting and how he'd
helped her get through the front door.

"And what does that have to do with him being
at your front door tonight?"

"A lost kitten." It sounded ridiculous to her,
too. From the look on Jane's face, it was obvious
she thought Ninna was putting her on as well.
"Honest."

Jane shot her a sceptical look, then snatched a second piece of pizza. "It sounds like the scary dude with the van asking a girl to help him find his lost puppy. Are you sure this guy is okay?"

With an outraged gasp, Ninna said, "Oh, now that's going too far. I think he brings animals home from the Center that need extra care or maybe a different kind of care. He said something about the kitten not doing so well in that clinical atmosphere."

"Obviously it wasn't enjoying itself at the vet's house either, not if it ran away first chance it got," Jane pointed out with a big smirk.

Ninna shook her head. "Anything could've happened. Kittens are curious and like to explore; they love to be outside too. Besides, rather than criticizing him, maybe we should go and look for the poor kitten."

Jane's gaze widened in disbelief. "So you *are* interested in him?"

"What? No! Of course not. I just met him today." Ninna could feel the heat rising on her cheeks, though. Damn Jane anyway. How did she always manage to get to the heart of something Ninna wanted to hide?

It's not that Ninna *was* interested...but... Okay, so maybe she was a little intrigued – or would be if she allowed herself to think about him that way. But she wasn't going to go there, because she needed this job, and office relationships weren't a good idea. She couldn't afford to lose her only pay check in six months. Besides he'd given her no real indication he was interested in her that way...

"So? Since when is that a reason not to stalk him."

"Stalk him? That's a horrible thing to suggest. I don't stalk people," Ninna gasped, outraged until Jane's laughter pealed through the room. "Oooh, you." Ninna threw her napkin at her. "That's it. We're forgetting what's important here... Let's go find a kitten." With that, Ninna stormed out the back door.

"No, wait. I'm not done eating. I was just kidding!" Jane hollered as she rose from the table.

Ninna ignored Jane's wails of distress and headed out through her backyard to the small white picket gate that separated her badly-in-need-of-a-cut grass from the alleyway behind her house. She didn't bother checking to see if her friend followed. Experience told her she would. Walking down the alleyway, she started meowing, hoping to have the kitten answer back. She couldn't imagine what anyone hearing her must think. She didn't really care.

"What are you doing?" Jane came up on her left.

"Here, kitty, kitty, kitty. Come here, kitty." Giving Jane a disgusted look, Ninna walked forward. "What do you think I'm doing?" A weak, plaintive cry sounded to her left. "What was that?" She turned to face Jane.

"What was what?" Jane stared blankly at her.

"Didn't you hear it? It sounded like a kitten crying." Ninna spun around. Other than a few rocks and the odd garbage can, there didn't appear to be any place for a kitten to hide.

Meow.

"It *is* a cat. Where is it?"

The two women searched everywhere. No luck. Then Ninna glanced through a picket fence to the backyard several houses away from hers. One of the rougher-looking houses that shared her alley but opened onto the next street. There, tucked up beside a stack of debris, was a tiny black kitten, its huge eyes glistening up at her.

"Oh, look at him. The poor thing," Jane said, staring down at it.

"He's scared." Slipping through the gate, Ninna picked him up.

"Good. Let's take him to your vet now. If it isn't his missing kitten, we can bring it back."

"I'm not bringing it back. Look where it is. This is no place for a baby of any kind." The two girls looked at the dilapidated back porch, with its sagging roof and the exterior badly in need of a paint job. "If it isn't the missing kitten, it's about to become Stuart's latest adoption." Casting a cautious eye at the house, Ninna backed out of the yard and into the alleyway. She closed the gate and turned to her friend. "Let's go. This place gives me the creeps."

Jane snorted. "It looks like a crack house. I wonder if it's deserted."

"Hopefully. It's not like deserted houses are unusual in today's economy. If I hadn't socked away as much money as I did, I'd have lost my place, too. Obviously, these people weren't so lucky." The kitten struggled in her arms, mewling in a horrible, high-pitched tone.

Jane ignored the tiny cries and carried on with the same conversation. "Yeah, you have a roof over your head, but your house is barely big enough for you. If you gain ten pounds, you'll have to move."

Trying to get a better grip on the kitten, Ninna snapped, "That's the only reason I could afford to buy it in the first place. Remember all those other over-priced places I considered first? If I'd bought one of those, I'd have lost it by now. Don't knock my home. It's small but cozy. Even better, it's mine."

They rounded the corner to enter the side street, leading them back onto the front of the same block. Ninna nodded toward the vet's huge house. "There's his place."

At the front door, Jane pressed on the doorbell. It pealed loudly and set off a cacophony of barking and yipping. Jane and Ninna looked at each other wide-eyed. "Holy crap. How many dogs does he have?" Jane's shocked voice was barely audible over the noise.

They could hear sounds of someone yelling at the dogs to be quiet. "Stop it. Move out of the way. How am I supposed to answer the door if you're all standing there?"

The door opened, and Stuart stood in front of them. He raised his eyebrows in surprise, but the surprise quickly morphed into pleasure. "Ninna?"

She couldn't help but feel an answering spark inside.

Then his gaze landed on the kitten, which was using Ninna's throat and collarbone as a monkey bar.

"Oh, you found him. That's wonderful." He opened the door wide. "Come in, please. Where was he?"

Stuart reached out to take the kitten from her, however the kitten had other plans and immediately dug in his claws.

Ninna winced. Her throat was going to look like she'd been the victim of a slasher attack. Eventually, with a little coaxing, the kitten let go and Ninna was able to swallow again. She said, "He was in the back alley, caught behind a pile of rubble in the yard of that deserted house almost at the end of the block." She glanced over at Jane then back to Stuart.

"This is my friend, Jane. She helped me find him."

Stuart smiled at Jane. "Hi, I'm Stuart. Thanks for helping out."

Jane beamed, obviously happy to discard the stalker scenario she'd suggested earlier.

"Please come in. Let me check him over quickly." He shut the front door and headed toward the back of the house. "Come back here. I have a room set up for the animals."

Ninna followed, amazed at the dogs bouncing around them. One had only three legs but it didn't appear to notice. A big Doberman was missing an ear, had a stumpy tail and his muzzle was scarred.

Ninna also noticed, but ignored, the basset hound. She avoided touching any of them, period. "You take in animals no one else wants, don't you?" she asked.

He glanced back, as if surprised by her question. Then noticed the dogs. "Occasionally. If they aren't going to be adopted out elsewhere, well...sometimes they need a break from the Center and I bring them home for a while."

"But once you do, it has to be hard to take them back?" she said, knowing it would be hard on her.

Jane piped up. "I'm surprised you're allowed this many in a private home."

"I'm not, really. My brother is building me a house on some acreage outside of town. But it'll be another month or two before I can move in. There will be lots of space for the animals there."

He entered a room that looked identical to a modified examining room at the Center. Walking around a large table, he carefully lowered the kitten onto it. It took only a few minutes to check the little furry body over. "Good. I'll give him some food and take him to his bed. He'll be just fine."

Stuart looked directly at Ninna, his gaze warming as he studied her. "Thank you. I wouldn't have wanted to lose him here, not when the new house is almost ready."

"He's going to love that."

Stuart grinned, his gaze taking in both women. "I don't know about him, but I sure will." He carried the kitten into the kitchen. Ninna, not sure what to do, followed. After he'd fed the kitten, he straightened. "Would you ladies like coffee? I'm sorry, I tend to focus on my four-legged friends and forget about the two-legged ones." He said it in such a boyish way Ninna couldn't help but be charmed.

"Thanks, I'd love one," Jane said.

Ninna glanced at Jane in surprise. She never drank coffee, but the look she flashed back at Ninna warned her not to say anything. Ninna's glance went from Jane to Stuart and back again.

Jane was giving him her best look-at-me-because-I'm-cute look. If it worked, fine. Any guy who fell for that kind of stupid stunt wasn't someone Ninna wanted for herself anyway.

Stuart didn't appear to notice Jane's attention-getting attempts. Bonus point in his favor. He turned and puttered around the gourmet kitchen. He seemed quite at home there.

"This is a great kitchen." Ninna studied the huge white oak cabinets. "Do you cook?"

"Sometimes. Being a bachelor, it is either learn to cook or live on take-out food." He shrugged. "So I learned." He flashed that shy grin Ninna's way and damned if her heart didn't go bump. "How about you?" he asked her.

Jane jumped in. "This kitchen is a dream. I love to cook, but I don't have anything as nice as this to cook in."

Ninna rolled her eyes. Talk about a misleading statement. Jane lived in a classy penthouse with the most beautiful gourmet kitchen Ninna had ever seen. Jane also couldn't cook worth a damn.

Ninna, on the other hand, loved to bake. Not that she should be doing any of that with her diet plans. She was a fair cook, but simple stuff, nothing fancy.

Several of the dogs moved through the kitchen. Ninna stiffened as the floppy basset hound entered. He looked just like the one from the Center. She eyed him carefully, but he ignored her to sniff the little kitten. The other dogs didn't appear to care. There was no fighting between the animals. All were well mannered.

"What about you, Ninna? Do you cook?"

She flushed, having been sidelined by the arrival of the basset hound. "I love to bake," she offered shyly.

–Cookies? I love cookies.

Ninna's gaze widened at the same damn voice. She glanced at the talking dog, realized it was staring at her, and hurriedly looked away. "I love to bake breads, actually. I don't bake many cakes or cookies."

–Pity.

"Not likely," she muttered softly.

–Hah, there you are. So glad you've decided to get over your snit and talk to me.

Against her better judgement, Ninna turned to look at the dog. His tongue lolled off to one side, as he panted deeply.

–I love cookies.

"You look it," she snapped, glaring at his rotund body. She turned her back on him. Both Stuart and Jane looked at her in astonishment. *Oh, shit.*

Embarrassed, she weakly tried to explain her outburst using old excuses she'd practiced years ago, "Sorry, I was replaying a conversation in my mind that hadn't gone so well yesterday. I guess I wish I'd said more than I did." Knowing her face was probably shining like a kid's hot pink glow stick, she mumbled, "It's time to head home. No time for coffee, sorry. Glad the kitten is going to be fine." She turned and raced to the front door.

God, how could she have done that?

She was such a loser.

Chapter 3

Ninna stormed home from Stuart's, cursing under her breath. Damn voices in her head. And she'd actually answered! Out loud, too, just to make it worse. What was wrong with her? Her hasty exit only amplified her idiocy. They'd really think she was ready for the looney bin. Maybe she was. Hadn't she considered it a few years ago?

Even if stress was the problem, she still had to deal with the fallout – the symptoms. Time to make that call to her shrink. She'd managed to put it out of her mind first with Jane and then the kitten incident, but no longer. Racing into her house, she slammed the front door.

She didn't bother to look to see if Jane followed. She had no illusions; Jane would continue to check out Stuart until he made his interest or disinterest known. Jane loved men, especially those who were the least interested in her. She could do with a shrink herself. They'd have a heyday with a woman who persisted in setting herself up for failure.

For herself, well, speaking aloud, to no one, about topics unrelated to the conversations going on around her…well, that definitely counted as nuts. She headed right to her bedroom where her address book sat in her night table drawer. Flicking to the end of the small leather-bound book, she located Dr. Theon's contact information. At one time, she'd known this number by heart.

She punched numbers so fast that she misdialed twice, but finally calmed down enough to get the sequence right.

Of course, she got his answering service. After relaying a message for him to please call her tonight, if possible, and if not, first thing in the morning, she closed her phone.

Then, for the first time since her outburst, she really breathed. Long slow breaths.

"Feel better?"

Glancing at Jane, who now leaned against the doorjamb, Ninna nodded. "Yes, I do. I know you don't like for me to go to the doctor, but I need to see him. I definitely don't want a relapse."

"And you won't have one if you stay calm."
Jane straightened up. "Come back out to the
kitchen. I'll put on the tea kettle."

Following meekly, Ninna allowed herself to be
talked into sitting down on the couch while her
friend warmed up another piece of pizza for
herself and brought Ninna a cup of tea.

"Are you seeing things again?"

There it was. Out in the open. "More like
hearing things."

"Maybe it was the pizza?" With a suspicious
eye, Jane studied the dripping hot piece of pizza
on the plate in front of her.

"No, it wasn't. It started this morning," Ninna
said, "as I walked into the Center."

Jane's face lit up and she snatched up the
pizza. "Easy, it was brought on by stress. You
were panicked about this job right from the
beginning."

Ninna sighed. She'd actually been anxious
about not finding a job for months. Still Jane was
right about one thing. Stressed – even panicked –
was exactly what she'd been this morning.
"Maybe, but I can't afford to lose this job, either.
This has to stop."

"So what if you are having a relapse?" Jane mumbled around dripping cheese. "You dealt with it before. You can do it again."

Ninna paused, staring at her friend. She was right. *She'd had a relapse.* That wasn't earth-shattering news. She'd had them before, recovered and had gone on. She *could* do it again.

Feeling better, she decided to enjoy her evening with her best friend. She also wanted to go a little deeper into Jane's reaction to Stuart. Not that Jane was going to get him.

Ninna had seen him first, after all. "So what did you think of Stuart?"

She was home. Troy ducked back around the corner of the small house, his jacket catching on the vinyl siding. Excitement sped through him as her shadow rippled on the other side of the thin curtains. She was in her bedroom, moving from one side of the room to the other. His imagination filled in the missing pieces. Those damn curtains were thicker than he wanted. Sheers would have been more convenient – for him. Damn, she was cute. Hot too.

He'd been here night after night, unable to help himself. Usually he didn't work the same area consecutive nights, but the lure of seeing her had him changing his pattern. He knew better. He'd stayed free of jail all these years by being careful and smart.

A burst of anger set him off. She was making him stupid. The longer he stood there, the more his warring emotions fought with him. She fascinated him. At the same time, he was taking risks and making mistakes he shouldn't.

If he got caught, it would be because of her.

Ignoring the dangers, he watched her shadow cross the room to her bed. She crawled under the covers and leaned up against the headboard. She was going to read.

Perfect. She did this every night.

He loved it when people followed the same pattern night after night.

It made his job so much easier.

***

Waking up in the middle of the night, Ninna wondered if the pizza had been a good idea after all. She stood up and raced to the bathroom.

Walking into her bedroom a few minutes later, she was uneasy. She realized the moon was hiding behind approaching storm clouds. Shivering at the gloomy night, she walked through her tiny house and double-checked the doors, windows and security system. All normal.

But it didn't feel normal. She felt tuned to some elusive danger. She couldn't quite place it, but something felt off and she knew one thing; there was no way she'd get back to sleep now. Grabbing a book, she propped herself against the headboard and started to read again.

But she couldn't settle into the story. Perhaps a change of book. She looked toward her desk, piled high with others – then she froze.

A shadow fell across her bedroom window. She shuddered and watched it closely. This was the one thing she hated about the house. Her bedroom was on the ground floor. Living alone just added to her nervousness. The shadow never moved. She stared at it, swallowing hard. Should she turn her light off? Or would that be worse? Was someone watching her house, or were the shadows and trees and the moonlight playing tricks on her?

There was nothing funny about this.

Throwing back her bedding, she slipped across the room to peer out the corner of her window. The shadow was there, but she couldn't see what created it. It moved suddenly, slipping around her house.

Her heart pounded and her stomach squeezed so tight she had trouble breathing. Oh God, please let it *not* be an intruder. She didn't know how to scare him off. The rash of break-ins in her neighborhood had all happened while home owners were away. Maybe if she made some noise to let him know there was someone inside, he'd leave.

Making a decision, she turned on the back porch light and watched as the shadow slunk away. She followed it from window to window, moving through the house until she couldn't see it anymore.

Whoever it was, had gone. As she dialed the police, shivers raced down her spine.

What if this guy came back?

***

The next morning before leaving for work, Ninna fought off her drowsiness with huge mugs of coffee. She needed another four hours of sleep, but had no chance of getting them. Her job was more important than sleeping.

Her arrival on the second day was easier. She was early and beat the crush she'd walked into the day before. She also entered through a different door. All of it helped to change her perspective and lessen her stress level. Coffee burbled as a fresh pot finished dripping. Grabbing a cupful, she headed to her desk, and almost smacked into Stuart.

He reached out and gently clasped her by the arms to steady her. "How are you feeling? Maybe you shouldn't have come in today."

Instead of stepping away, she leaned back slightly to look up into his face. *What was he talking about?* Her confusion must have shown, because he added, "After you ran out last night, Jane explained how you'd been feeling sick earlier."

Oh she had, had she? Funny, Jane hadn't told Ninna about that conversation and they'd covered the subject of Stuart pretty intensely. And Jane had explained she only stayed to check out Stuart – for Ninna's sake. That was so Jane.

"I'm feeling much better. Still a little tired, though," she added. Hopefully, that gave her an excuse for the bags under her eyes that no amount of makeup would cover.

"You take it easy today. If you start to feel unwell, consider leaving early."

Ninna smiled. "Thanks for the sentiment, but I need this job. Sick or not."

He frowned. "I understand. However, we don't want anyone else getting sick, especially anyone working around the animals."

Right. So his concern was for everyone else, not really for her. *Figures*. Still he was right. Sigh. She plastered a cheerful smile on her face. "No worries. I'm much better. Not contagious, I guarantee." As he hadn't dropped his hands, she stepped back and then headed around him to her desk.

Once there, she sat down and attempted to read through her training notes of the day before, which was not an easy thing to do as a continuous stream of animals arrived – on her side of the counter. Did everyone in this place bring their animals to work? Some employees arrived with dogs, one had a cat in a small basket, and someone had a parrot or something similar on his shoulder – now that guy was going to leave a mess.

"It's okay, Ninna, we don't do this every day," Stacey said from behind her, startling her.

"Sorry, I didn't hear you come in." Ninna kept her hand to her chest, waiting for her heart to stop galloping inside. "What were you saying?"

"I was trying to explain the animals. Today is staff clinic day. Anyone who has a pet that needs to see a vet can bring it in free of charge. One of the benefits of working here. It happens once a month." She grinned at Ninna. "Do you have a pet?"

Ninna chuckled as she finally understood what was happening around her. "No. I've thought about it, but hadn't felt the need."

"If you live alone, a dog can be a great companion, not to mention a wonderful guard dog."

That reminded her of her shadowy visitor the previous night. "Maybe, you're right," she said slowly. "I have been nervous these last few nights. The recent break-ins in my neighbourhood have been kind of scary."

"There you go." Stacey walked toward her office. "If you decide that's something you'd like to look into further, talk to Stuart. He'd be happy to help you decide on the perfect breed."

"I'll think about it."

"Think about what?" Stuart walked toward her, a huge puppy in his arms. "Did you see this guy? He's only three months old."

Ninna's gaze widened and she gasped in delighted horror. "What? He's huge!"

"He's a Newfoundland puppy. Belongs to one of our trainers."

Ninna wanted to walk over and give the overgrown teddy bear a cuddle, only she wasn't quite to that point...yet. "He's gorgeous," she whispered in delight from behind her desk. "So many animals today."

"There always are lots. Today, though, they are also on your side of the counter."

She smiled. Maybe she should get a dog, although she'd have to buy a bigger house for one like this baby. "Stacey explained why there are extra animals here today. She also suggested I speak with you about what kind of dog might be good for me, if I can even get comfortable enough with the idea to take that step."

He raised an eyebrow. "Do you have any pets?"

When she shook her head, he frowned. "Then why a dog? Maybe a cat is better. They generally require less maintenance, don't have to be taken out for walks, and can be left alone for longer periods of time."

"I'm not sure what I want," she admitted.

She still mulled it over when the basset hound walked around the corner in the company of a black lab. She eyed him carefully, glad she was sitting with the desk safely between them. He sat down on his wrinkly butt and grinned at her.

"A cat might be nice," she said cautiously, never taking her eye off the dog staring at her.

The dog's grin widened.

She shuddered and looked away.

"A cat can be great company if you're a cat person. If you're not, well, let's just say that you shouldn't go there."

That brought a startled laugh out of her. "Then I guess I should put some more thought into it."

"True. And consider that a dog has a function in your home. They can be great watchdogs. Look at all the break-ins in our neighborhood this last week. A dog might have prevented those."

"Or the dog would have been injured by the intruders." She'd feel terrible if that happened.

Stuart shook his head. "That's why we're such strong advocates of training here. True, if the intruders had a gun, a bullet is definitely going to do a lot of damage to a dog. But a good dog is going to do a lot of damage to an intruder, too. Often just the presence of a watchdog is enough to stop the intruder from even trying. Why bother? There are easier houses to go after."

"So you're saying they're really a deterrent?" She got that, and after last night's scare, she wouldn't mind taking one home at the end of the day, for that reason alone. "I was afraid someone was watching my house last night."

"Really? I thought I heard someone around the garage last night too, but after the initial noise alerted the dogs, I couldn't hear anything but them. Needless to say, if there were an intruder, he didn't stay around long." He shifted the dog's weight in his arms. Huge chocolate eyes peered up at him curiously, waiting for the jostling to be over.

She laughed. "He's so content."

"Nothing bothers this little guy. But he's too big for you. A lab would be better. They make great family dogs. A small dog might be a good choice, too. They can be yappy, though.

"Right. More to think about. Do you do adoptions here?"

"Absolutely. Matching the right dog to the right person is important." He started to walk back down the hallway. "When you get a moment, come to the back and see the various animals we have there."

"I will." She wasn't sure she wanted a dog at this stage of her life. Why couldn't she just borrow one for a while? See how that worked out first? She pondered that concept as she turned back to her work. Surely that was an option? Didn't centers foster animals out?

"Yes we do," Stuart answered, at the end of her work day when she finally managed to approach him with the question. "Usually, though, they're animals with special needs and are matched to caregivers who have the time and love for them."

He pointed at several cages behind her. "For example, the calico cat in the first cage…her front leg was badly damaged when she was brought in. We had to amputate it. Now she's on the mend and will finish her recovery at a foster home. She'll most likely go to Nancy, a retired nurse.

When the wound has healed, the cat will be put up for adoption."

"So I can't 'try out' a dog?" She winced at the look Mosey gave her as he sidled past to a large cushion by the back door. "I know that probably sounds wrong, but I just don't know that I'm going to like having a dog around."

He stared at her thoughtfully. "I have a suggestion for you. I have to go away next weekend. Why don't you look after my dogs? Even better, stay in the spare room. That way, you'll have some idea of what to expect when living with them. Dogs are great company," he added warmly. "Besides, you'd be doing me a huge favor."

She sighed. "I'm a sad case, huh?"

A boyish grin split his face. "No, you're cautious. That's a good thing. We don't want you adopting a dog and then finding out that the two of you aren't a good fit."

"So in a week and a half?"

"I'm leaving on the Friday. My brother had planned to help out, but he's finishing up with contractors on my acreage and it would be inconvenient for him to stay in town then."

"When are you coming back?"

"As early as I can on Sunday, probably noonish. In theory, you'd only be there for two nights. You can go back and forth to your house as you need to. I'd prefer you stay over instead of just coming back and forth to feed them. With as many animals as there are, they'll be much calmer if they have someone with them all the time."

She gave in. It was her fault, really. She'd asked and this had been his solution. It wasn't a bad one, and it was for only a couple of days. Besides, she'd be helping him out. That would be a good thing – right?

Then he did it.

"As a thank you, I'd love to take you out for dinner after I get back. I know a great Thai restaurant downtown." His wheedling tone made her grin. He sounded like a twelve-year-old boy trying to get his own way.

She relented, secretly delighted, but not wanting him to see how much she loved the idea of the date. Jane would laugh or if she'd been lying about her own lack of interest in Stuart – she'd be pissed. Still, Ninna knew Stuart wasn't Jane's type. "Fine, but you have to make a list of everything I have to do for the dogs. Make it so an eight-year-old could understand. I've never been around dogs, so I don't know when they have to go for walks or anything."

His face lit up. "No problem. I'll make sure the instructions are easy enough the dogs could follow them."

Shaking her head at her own stupidity for agreeing to dog sit, she walked out to her car. "Damn, what did I just do?"

—Hot dog! We're gonna have fun next weekend.

Ninna stopped and looked around.

Mosey lay on the grass beside a cherry-red Jeep with a roll bar instead of a roof. So, Stuart drove a Jeep. *Nice.*

—If you ask nice, he'll take you for a ride.

"I'm not talking to you. Go away." Determined not to pay attention, she continued walking to her blue Honda Civic.

—Never again. Now that I've found you, I'm never going to give you any peace!

Chapter 4

Ninna managed to forget about the upcoming weekend for over a week. That had been made all the easier as the basset hound communication seemed to have stopped. It must have been the stress of the new job. It had taken a few days of looking over her shoulder and eyeing dogs a little warily, but finally she'd relaxed. She could do this. And maybe even enjoy it.

Then Friday rolled around, and her calm disappeared. Because it *was* today that she'd promised to help Stuart out. *Damn it.* Why had she decided to do this? An offer to help a friend was one thing. An offer to help a sexy, eligible guy was another thing. To deal with dogs, including a potential talking dog, now that was a different story altogether.

It was stupid, but she was working herself up into a real lather over looking after a few animals for a couple of days. How hard could it be? Feed them, change their water. She even considered staying in her house and just checking on them a couple of times. No biggie.

This was ridiculous. Just thinking about it turned her into a frazzled witch as the week wore on.

"Hey Ninna, have you finished updating the reports?" Stacey walked toward her desk with a large stack of papers in hand.

"Yes, but I haven't printed them off yet." Ninna got up to check that the printer had paper. "Do you need them right now?"

"No need, as long as I have them by the end of the day." Stacey, with an already-on-to-the-next-problem look on her face, strode off, leaving Ninna wondering if everyone was having a bad day.

—Of course they are. Budget cuts and grant deadlines. Human stuff.

Ninna stiffened. All week she'd managed to avoid the basset hound, keeping her head down and her mind closed. Not an easy feat. It was something she'd learned how to do years ago. Focus on one thing only. Don't get sidetracked by non-essentials. She thought it had been working – until now.

—It wasn't working all week, either. I thought you could use some time. You know...to get used to having me around.

She turned very slowly. Mosey sat in a slumped sitting position, his wrinkles arguing with gravity as they slowly settled down toward his tail. Ninna couldn't help backing up slightly. She was fascinated by him. She'd never been this close to his breed...and didn't plan to get any closer. She'd made wide circles around the dog to avoid accidentally coming into contact with him. He creeped her out, unlike some of the other breeds she'd been happy to touch and cuddle. All those wrinkles...they so weren't working for her. She shuddered.

Many animals were foreign to her. Two weeks on the job hadn't been enough to change that. She *wanted* to be an animal person, and cuddling the kitten she'd returned to Stuart had felt good. Yet she knew from experience that wanting something didn't make it so, at least not overnight.

Dogs still made her uncomfortable. She could probably blame that on Mosey for the moment.

—Are you done yet? You keep going around in circles. Get over yourself.

Ninna lifted her head and stared at him. "Easy for you to say. You're obviously comfortable around people."

—*Why not? It's people that feed me, walk me and give me rides in cool vehicles.*

Ninna stared. "That's it? That's the only thing you think about? Your comfort?"

Mosey's front legs slid out from under him, and he dropped the rest of the way to the floor.

—*What else is there?*

The milk chocolate-colored wrinkles on his back jiggled back and forth like pudding before coming to a slow stop. She shook her head to remove that image. "Lots," she snapped.

"Sorry, Ninna. Did you say something?" Stuart stopped in front of her, a puzzled look on his face.

Heat crept up over her face. "Just talking to myself again," she muttered. With a heavy sigh, she added, "Sorry, it's a bad habit."

He grinned. "No problem. It's kinda cute, actually." With that stunning remark, he returned to one of the many rooms in the back. Even after all this time at the Center, her radar flashed on every time he came and went, like a traffic light. She was an idiot.

So he thought talking to herself was cute, huh?

–Get over it. He will.

She gasped. "Oh, that's *so* mean."

–Whatever. Mosey rolled onto his side, his breath gusting out in a heavy movement. His jowls appeared to re-form into a grin. Ninna shuddered. She *was* an idiot. Somehow she'd found it easier to speak to a talking dog than to relax about looking after him. Or were the nerves due to the promise of her future date with Stuart?

Stupid.

–Yeah. You're not kidding.

"Oh, shut up." Lifting her head, she spun around, hoping no one else had heard her. Thankfully the open office was empty. "You're making me crazy."

–Can't make something that already is.

Her back stiffened and she glared at Mosey. The last thing she needed was to have a dog, or anyone, call her crazy. Bad enough she thought it herself.

Stuart returned to her desk. "So can I give you a lift home tonight? I noticed you've been walking to work lately. I'll need to get moving as soon as I show you around and give you the instructions. I'd hoped to have more time, but it's not looking good at this point."

Ninna tore her eyes off Mosey and stared at Stuart, mentally trying to shift to the new topic. *He'd noticed her walking?* Right. This weekend. He was leaving...

She swallowed. "Sure." Checking the clock, she realized it was quitting time. "Are you sure you want to leave your animals in my hands? I really don't know what I'm doing."

He flashed her that devilish grin and her heart sighed. "What better way for you to learn than to give this a try? You're thinking about getting a dog, so this is perfect."

She winced. "I wish those damn break-ins would stop. I don't think I slept at all last night."

"Tonight you will. The dogs will keep any intruders at bay."

She glanced at the two dogs at his side. The three-legged one didn't appear to notice his disability. He ran around the same as the other. Mosey should be the one running. He might lose a pound or two.

–Exactly why I don't. I'm perfect the way I am.

She glared at him, then remembered herself, and quickly switched on a smile. "Maybe."

"I'm offering a good night's sleep," Stuart wheedled. "You won't be sorry. And if you sleep over at my house, the animals are calmer."

She stood up and grabbed her windbreaker and purse. "Except there is nothing like sleeping in your own bed."

"True, if you're actually sleeping."

There was no way to argue with that.

Stuart motioned to the back door. "Let's go this way and I'll lock up as I go." As he talked he checked the various locks and doors.

"Are break-ins a problem here?" It surprised her as she watched him check the security so closely. She'd never expected an animal clinic to have issues like that.

He shot her a frustrated look. "We keep drugs on hand. There's always a problem with junkies. Unfortunately, it's like anywhere else. Where's there's opportunity, there will be people to take advantage."

Before she'd realized it, they were standing in front of his Jeep. He unlocked her side, then opened his door and let the dogs into the back. She hopped in and struggled with the seatbelt. Considering there was no roof, she definitely wanted to be buckled in, even if the drive was only a few blocks.

Stuart did a lot of running around, so it made sense for him to drive to work daily. For herself, walking to work meant fresh air, exercise, a chance to relax and unwind, and it saved gas money. Now that she'd successfully concluded her first two weeks at her new job, she'd settled into a routine. At least no axe had fallen on her head for screwing up. That was good, but it would take longer for her to feel like she really belonged.

"I'll drive straight home, if you don't mind. After I show you around, you can run home and get anything you might need for an overnight stay." He grinned at her. "I kinda like the idea of you sleeping in my house."

She rolled her eyes at his nudge to stay overnight. And her insides fluttered at his innuendo. He did have a point, though about this weekend. A good night's sleep would be wonderful.

"Sure, I can do that." Even as she said that, Stuart pulled into his driveway. He pushed a button on his visor and the garage door lifted. Pulling in, he parked and hopped out while she was still looking for the seatbelt release.

Getting out slowly, she waited for Stuart to open the door to the house. As soon as he pushed it open, a small white dog, something like a hairy dachshund, ran out.

"That one is Goober." Stuart hit a switch by the door, closing the garage door. "He loves everyone, but he gets overexcited when I take him into the Center so I usually leave him home."

"Hi, Goober," she said, then turned to Stuart. "I don't remember seeing him last time." Ninna couldn't resist bending over to scratch the wiggling white bundle as it did its best to trip her up. Maybe she was loosening up a bit, at least around the small breeds.

Ninna followed Stuart inside. Once again, she was hit by the sheer vastness of the house compared to her little nugget. She loved her home, but had to admit it was on the snug side. Jane was right. This place would hold three houses like hers.

"Sorry if the place is messy. I've been rushed to get ready for my trip. Normally, I bring the housecleaning service in on the weekend, but I didn't want to have that as another thing for you to look after."

Housecleaning service? Was he nuts? No, just single, male and with a hell of a lot more money than she had. And, she had to admit that with all the animals, a cleaning service was just plain sensible.

Stuart led her into the kitchen where he handed her a list of instructions. While she read, he rattled them off the top of his head. "The dogs get fed twice a day. There's dry kibble here in the pantry." He opened the door and showed her. "Once a day, I open a can and split it amongst their bowls. Put the dry kibble in first, then the can, then add some water and stir everything up. That way they'll lick the bowl clean. Not that it's much of a problem with dogs. You can see on the paper, I have down two amounts here. One amount for the larger two and a smaller amount for the rest. Give the larger dogs their bowls first then the smaller ones. Don't worry if one doesn't clean it all up. I can guarantee you that the other dogs will finish it."

He rambled on about the dog's routines, including feeding and exercise. Ninna tried to file his words away, knowing she'd forget the minute he left. Thank heavens he'd written it all down. How hard could this be?

—Not. Just don't forget my double portions. I gotta keep my figure.

Ninna refused to face Mosey, and focused instead, on Stuart's rapid-fire instructions.

"Now for the two kittens—"

"Two?"

"Yes, there's Blackster here and his new friend..." Stuart picked up a little kitten sleeping in a cushion-type basket she hadn't even seen. "This guy is Tiny. He's another runt and exceptionally small for his age. He's doing fine and with a few months of good food, he's liable to outgrow his siblings."

Ninna couldn't resist cooing over the miniature bundle. She'd never seen anything so adorable. Not black, not brown, but some mottled mix of colors. On top of that, he had huge eyes. "He's gorgeous." She placed the list on the counter and reached out to take the little kitten. "You're making me realize what I've missed all my life."

"Every child should have a family pet. It's an American tradition."

Ninna laughed. "That was the problem, then. My parents were killed in a small plane crash, so I lived with my aunt from the age of six. She had allergies. More than that, she was very stern and strict. Animals would never have been allowed inside."

His grin widened. "Now you have all weekend to make up for it and decide what you'd like to have in your own home."

Ninna smiled as a warm spot in her heart grew. Tiny yawned, and she saw the same mottled color inside his mouth. "This guy is definitely adoptable."

"All kittens are. Our problem at the Center stems from having too many adult cats. They're old enough to have lost their cuteness, but young enough they have a lot of years of love left to give. It's this age group that can fill a shelter. Then there are the old timers – cats that are over eight years old that still have years left. No one wants them because they *are* older."

Ninna dropped a gentle kiss on Tiny's head and returned him to Stuart's hands. After that, it was a fast trip though the house, which was starting to look more as a pet facility, as it included two birds in a cage, and...oh gross, a snake. From the doorway Ninna gaped at the reptile in a glass cage and refused to enter the room.

Stuart laughed. "I just wanted you to know this guy is here. He's been fed and is good until I get back."

Ninna tilted her head as she stared at the sunning snake with revulsion. "Good thing, because I'd have been out of here, otherwise."

"He has a cut on his back. It's healing and I have this perfect window with a great balance of sun and shade for him."

"Lucky him," she muttered, backing up and out of the room.

With a chuckle, he grabbed her arm and urged her toward the staircase. "Upstairs is your bedroom. Look on this as a weekend away."

Ninna refrained from answering. At the second floor, Stuart opened a door to a large guest bedroom. Huge windows overlooked the street. She had to admit, sleeping higher than the ground floor would be nice for a change. She remembered the shadowy figure from the night before… How would she manage to go back to her house again if she let fear beat her?

—And what's wrong with a mini holiday?

Recognizing the voice, Ninna hunched her shoulders. At least she had the foresight to not answer.

"Everything you need should be here. I've put several towels on the dresser for you." He checked his watch as he finished speaking, concern wrinkling his features. "I'm sorry, but I have to run to catch my plane. The seminar is over Sunday afternoon, so I should be back by nine that night. I promise I'll get home as fast as I can."

She trailed behind him as he went downstairs, only now noticing the packed suitcase by the front door. He went over the simple security system then turned to face her.

"You'll be fine. What's your cell phone number?" He pulled a cell phone and entered the number she reeled off and told her he added it to his list of contacts. "Good. I'll call you in the morning." He pulled out a small notebook and wrote something down before ripping it off and giving it to her. "This is where I'm staying and this is my cell. Call me if you need me. If I can't answer right away, I'll get back to you as soon as I can."

He studied her for a brief moment. He must have seen the panicked look on her face, because he said, "You'll be fine, honest. And thanks, I really appreciate you helping me out."

He surprised her with a light kiss on her cheek, and with that, he was gone. Ninna stood in the doorway with the dogs milling around her legs, until Stuart reversed down the driveway and took off around the corner of the block. The garage door closed automatically, giving an added oomph to the sense of loneliness she felt in the huge house.

–Great, so now what? A walk? A brushing? I know, how about some dinner?

Ninna glared down at Mosey. "How about none of those? How about I go back to my place and try to forget about you guys for an hour or so, huh? How does that sound?"

–Sounds cowardly to me. With those words, the oversized Mosey did his famous slumping act to the tiled floor.

–Oh, I'm so hungry. Feed me! Feed me!

Walking into her own home a half hour later, Ninna dropped off the lunch containers she had stashed in her oversized purse. After being in Stuart's home, her house appeared tiny and more cramped than ever. A good night's sleep in the guest room across the street was very tempting, and the dogs probably did better with company. After all, she did, so it made sense they would, too.

Changing into jeans and t-shirt helped her relax and slip into the whole 'I'm home after a day at the office' feeling. As grateful as she was for the job, it was just a job. Grabbing her latest mystery book from the library, she threw together a small overnight bag, locked up and headed to Stuart's house. He had a huge TV, comfy circular couch and animals for company. She'd be stupid not to take advantage.

When she'd crossed the road, she'd been amazed at the view from his side of the street. From her side, she could only see the large wealthy homes. From his side of the street, looking across at her house and neighbours it presented the poster picture for that old saying of living on the wrong side of the tracks.

The dogs started barking as she walked up the driveway. Even though she knew how many dogs were inside, their barks made her steps falter. She couldn't imagine an intruder thinking Stuart's house was worth the trouble, not when her side of the street offered so much easier access. Then again, her side of the street probably offered less in profits too.

Unlocking the front door and actually getting past the wiggling bodies was another trick. The dogs were hungry and probably needed to go for their walk soon. She shouldn't have drawn out her visit home.

—*Ya think? The next time you need to go to the bathroom, we'll make you wait another hour before you get to go.*

Embarrassed by his comment, she headed into the kitchen and the food dishes. Opening the kitchen door, she let the dogs out into the backyard then she sorted out their meals. Grabbing her instruction list, she doled out the food to the dogs, then the cats and the birds. She refused to open the door to the room that housed the snake. When she was finished, she walked into the spare bedroom she'd been offered. That's when she saw it – an attached bathroom with a Jacuzzi tub.

That was it. Decision made. She'd holiday here for the night.

***

Hours later, she realized getting to sleep hadn't been a problem, but getting *back* to sleep after waking up proved to be. Ninna checked the MP3 player she'd brought with her. *Just after 2:00 in the morning.* She groaned. *I hate waking up in the middle of the night. Hate it, hate it, hate it!* She rolled over and pulled the covers over her shoulders. The downside of being in the huge house was the chill factor. It was summer, but the nights were cool. In her little house, the heat stayed fairly constant. *Not here.*

Lying there, she realized another problem. She had to go to the bathroom. *Damn.*

Hopping up, she raced to the bathroom. When she finished, she walked back just as quickly. Almost to the bed, she veered off to look out the window. The moonlight, peeking through the clouds, shone down on the street. Walking to the next window, she studied the area and picked out her own little house on the right. She smiled. It looked cute like that.

Then she saw *it.*

Movement.

Around the front of her house, a shadow slid along the wall to where her bedroom window was. Her heart pounded. *Shit. Was that an intruder?*

Was her house being broken into just because she'd decided to spend the night here?

—Boy, are you stupid. What if you were home right now? This guy would be watching you sleep. Or worse.

Ninna spun around to see Mosey standing in her doorway. "What do you mean?"

—What if he's not trying to break in?

Ninna shook her head. As she watched, Mosey lifted a back leg to scratch his rib and lost his balance. "What do you know? You're just a chubby dog."

—A chubby watch dog, thank you.

She glared at him. "The only thing you guard is your damn food dish."

—Go ahead and make fun of me. See if I care. The intruder isn't walking around my house, looking for me.

"Looking for me?" Ninna spun to look back out the window, horrified at the concept. "It can't be. We've had a run of break-ins in the neighbourhood. Everyone knows that."

—Of course they do.

"He'd have no reason to be looking for me. I'm nobody. I'm not even particularly good looking."

—Well, I know that.

She gasped at the insult, turning to glare at him.

—But you live alone and you're female. Bad combination.

"Says who? You're just a dog, and a big, fat, old, lazy one at that." Ninna couldn't believe the words blurting off her tongue. She never talked like this. She always went out of her way to be nice.

—Yeah, then you met me. If a dog could laugh, that's what he was doing now.

Laughing. At her.

She felt ashamed of herself. He was an animal, one she was supposed to look after, not verbally abuse.

—True enough. Best make up for it before I tell Stuart. More food works.

"Tell Stuart? You can talk to him, too?" Ninna brightened, loving that idea. How cool would that be if they could both talk to dogs?

—Nah, not really. But he's really good at reading us, so we make out fine. Besides, it's not like you're talking to just any dog, you're talking to me.

A loud noise sounded outside. The tinkling sound rippled through the darkness as she stared out into the night. Dogs barked in the distance. Mosey joined her at the window, jumping up so his big knotty paws landed on the window ledge. He woofed once – really loud.

She stared at him in shock. She didn't think he had it in him.

–Told you. The alert guard dog woofed again.

The house woke up as all the dogs came to the guest room, running and barking. She'd left her bedroom door ajar, thinking it might help her hear the animals if they needed anything. Now her room filled with excited canines.

She grabbed up her cell phone and dialled 911.

"Gee, thanks. Like I needed all of you here," she muttered to Mosey as she waited for someone to answer. The dogs roamed the room, barking and sniffing at everything. "And how come they can't talk like you can?"

He sniffed. She glared at him. He did it again. What dog could make a sound like a stifled sneeze moving through gravy?

–Gravy? Yum, I love gravy. Can we have gravy for breakfast?

"911, what is your emergency?"

Ninna quickly explained the situation. After giving her name, number and location – boy, she couldn't believe how long it took to make an emergency call – she hung up. Someone would come and check out the disturbance. She just hoped that someone came fast. What if she were in her own bed right now? What if a burglar was walking off with her valuables? Not that she had much, but still... A person could die while waiting for the police to check this out.

–Gravy. It's morning, right? Food time. Walk time.

"No! It's not morning, it's not time for breakfast...and there's no way in hell you're getting gravy."

–Gravy, oh I love gravy! Mosey spun around in a circle of joy – and became sidetracked by his tail. Ninna laughed as he chased it halfway around the room. The boxer yelped. The big black three-legged lab took the opportunity to lie down beside the bed and go to sleep while the Doberman woofed several times. The smaller white dog, Goober, persisted at the window, barking his head off at the moon.

Such chaos and noise. Why had she thought having a dog would be a good idea?

Off in the distance, she could hear other dogs picking up the serenade and howling together. Did they have a doggie telegraph or something?

Still, there was no sign of a cruiser or the sound of sirens blaring to scare off intruders. Then did she want him scared off or caught? If not caught tonight, he could return when she was home alone again.

She winced, not liking the sound of that. After what she'd just seen, she might never sleep in her bed again.

–Stay here, then. Move in with Stuart. He needs a girlfriend. A big happy family. Mosey panted at her feet, his chest moving so heavily she was afraid he'd have a heart attack.

–I could get used to gravy for breakfast.

Where was she? She should be here. That she wasn't, made his skin run hot and anger burn deep inside. She couldn't have a boyfriend. Maybe she went out of town, but that would break the pattern he'd followed for months. She could have stayed at a girlfriend's house. That would make sense.

But not really.

Anger built. *Damn it.* Why wasn't she here? He stood outside her bedroom window. The curtains were partly open, enough to see the hastily tossed clothes on the undisturbed bed. She'd come home and left again instead of sleeping in her own bed. He slipped around the back to her garage. Her car was there. Stumped, he leaned against the wall and considered the options. She could have been picked up for the evening then stayed over. Or she could have walked to wherever she was now. No way to tell.

At least from the garage.

He walked over to the inside door. Locked and secured. He could disarm it and have the door open in minutes.

Excitement rippled at the thought of going in and seeing how she lived. Walking around her bedroom, checking her closets and drawers. Peering into her life… He'd already checked her mail several times. But he wanted more. The risks would be tenfold compared to what he'd done so far. He didn't need that. He didn't want to go back to jail.

But he wanted her. *Ninna.*

***

When Ninna opened her eyes the next morning, she moaned and slammed them closed again. What a horrible night. The cops had arrived at her door not long after the call and told her what she'd expected to hear. They hadn't found anyone casing the neighborhood, but they would continue to patrol the area. She'd had them do a quick 'go around' of Stuart's yard before they left.

Then she'd tried to go back to sleep. It had taken forever. She'd allowed the dogs to sleep in her room for an added sense of security.

Probably not the wisest idea. All of them had somehow managed to hop up onto her bed. Beside her and half on her, every square inch of the double bed was covered in a canine blanket. *What was up with that?* Even the little white barking thing, Goober, had taken up residence on her spare pillow. She tried to roll over, and groaned. She couldn't budge with them holding the damn covers down.

Her phone rang at that moment. Struggling upright, she reached across doggie paws and heads to snag it from her night table, where she'd put it after her early morning call to the police.

"Good morning, Ninna. How did you make out last night?"

Stuart. Her tummy warmed and the smile on her face was so wide, she felt like a schoolgirl with her first crush. "Hi, good to hear you arrived safely. My night, yeah, that was interesting." She gave him the rundown on the nocturnal neighborhood activity.

"Then I'm very glad to hear you stayed at my house." His warm concern was a comfort after her frazzled night.

"I was too, until I woke up this morning. Why didn't you warn me about the dogs being bed hogs?"

Stuart's warm laughter reached through the phone and made her toes curl. "I never thought about it. I gather you left your door open?"

She grinned, staring at her bed again. The big black lab had stretched across the entire place where a second person would lie. Goober hadn't moved. He, or was it she, snuffled and tucked its head in deeper. "You would not believe my bed right now. I can barely move."

"You're still in bed?" His voice deepened and a whole new element entered. God, he was sexy.

She murmured back, willing to play, "I am. You've deputized your dogs as my bed mates."

"Ha! I'm coming home early then. Damn, are they *all* there?"

She sighed as the boxer kicked his legs out, shifting her own heavier legs against the lab. "Oh, yeah, they are all here." Mosey had sprawled along the bottom of the bed, lying on his back, all four feet pointed to the ceiling, grinning at her. She was so not going there.

"Good thing you're just a little bit of a thing. Otherwise there'd be no room."

She snickered. "There *is* no room. I forgot the lab's name, but he's taking up half the bed himself."

"That's Ticker. He used to belong to an older guy who passed away. Ticker spent the bulk of his life alone and didn't adapt well to the noise and confusion at the Center. That's why he goes in daily to learn social skills."

"Hmm. So when are you coming home?"

"I was due to speak tomorrow, but they've shifted things around and now my talk is today. I'm scheduled to stay overnight, but home is sounding pretty damn good right now." His voice deepened again, leaving innuendos hanging in the air. "I won't be able to make a decision until I see if I'm expected to attend tomorrow. Otherwise, I might leave after dinner. I'd still be very late, if I make it at all, though, so please stay. I like the idea of you sleeping in my house, my bed."

There it was again, that deeply sexual undertone that headed straight to her libido. "I'm sleeping in your spare bed not in *your* bed," she teased.

"For the moment. Think of me today."

He rang off, leaving her staring down at the phone in her hand. How could she not stay the night after that comment? Of course, that's exactly why he'd done it.

–*Gravy time?*

"No gravy for you. You should be on a diet. Look at you – your rolls almost kiss the ground when you walk." She struggled to sit up, shifting dogs as necessary.

–*More to love. Diets are a human issue. What animals would willingly deprive themselves of what they love?*

"People are health conscience. You should be, too." Speaking of which, breakfast sounded good to her. She hoped Stuart had something decent in the fridge. She hadn't even looked last night because she'd scarfed a quick bite at her house.

—Exactly. Gravy? It's one of the main food groups.

She stared down at Mosey. "You're a joke. Besides there isn't any gravy in the house."

—You can make some. Stuart does.

He does?" She loved the idea of man who could cook. "Maybe I do need to get to know him better."

Mosey nodded his head, jowls flapping in the windy movement. She had to laugh. If he'd been human he'd be a stand-up comic.

—If I were human, I'd be eating gravy.

Chapter 5

Ninna shooed the dogs off the bed and headed downstairs where she let them out into the yard. After a shower and a slow getting-dressed session, Ninna made up the bed. She didn't know if she'd be sleeping here again tonight or not. Last night had been a unique experience. She'd slept with several two-legged animals over the course of her relationships, but never four-legged ones.

Downstairs, she grabbed her instructions and doled out breakfast, then called the dogs in. The feeding of the dogs went faster this time and she felt more comfortable with the dogs' antics. When Tiny finished his meal, she couldn't resist picking him up and taking her cup of tea to the living room for an extended cuddle. He didn't appear to mind.

Sitting there, she had an insight into a world she'd never considered before. With a pet, there was someone to cuddle, someone to talk to, someone for company. On crappy days, you *had* to get up to look after a pet, because, as she was learning, pets require care. They gave you purpose in life.

She supposed it might sound sad to other people to hear about someone like her, twenty-six, employed and single, without a ton of friends – most had moved away in the last year. She wasn't a huge fan of the social networking sites either. She'd prefer to have friends close by to do things with. However, as she wasn't overwhelmed with too many of those, a pet or two might be nice – two, because then they'd have each other for company if she went out.

–*Walk. It's walk time.* Mosey planted himself in front of her.

"But I haven't eaten yet."

–*Too bad, so sad. We need to go for a walk.*

"Crap." But she got up, took Tiny back to his basket and headed out the back door.

The dogs burst out the door, tails wagging and noses in the air, happy to check out the world. They started their regular day with more enthusiasm than she did on a good day. She stood in the sunshine, drinking her tea while the dogs explored.

Ten minutes later, she was pulled out of her peaceful reverie.

—That's great. Now it's time to go for a walk. We need our exercise.

"I can't take all of you for a walk at the same time. That is not going to work. You guys will drag me all over the place."

She remembered something about that in Stuart's instructions. She went back inside and snatched up what amounted to her animal care bible. "So Brie, the boxer, and Goober, the white mop, require leashes but the rest are good and stay close." She snickered. "Like I'm going to believe that."

—You should. We go out all the time.

"Okay. I'm willing, definitely not eager, but let's take a walk over to my house and see if that guy caused any damage last night. If everyone behaves, I'll consider a trip to the park afterwards."

—The park. The park. We're going to the park.

As she grabbed up the leashes, excitement swept through the dogs. She decided to follow Stuart's instructions and take them out together, but if the first experiment went wrong, it would be relays until he returned.

Two dogs came running at the sound of the leash chains. She presumed they were the right ones as there were no other takers. By the time she had the two leashed, all were twisting and wiggling with joy. At least she was making *them* happy.

She opened the front door, and all the dogs jumped outside barking. Great. Now the neighbors were going to be mad at her for making so much noise. She walked slowly so the dogs could do their thing, sniffing and wandering around as they were wont to do. And was Mosey rolling in the grass? She hoped not. She kept walking, but looked back when she'd gone forward a dozen feet. He still lay there.

"Mosey, come on."

–Why? It's nice here.

"No, it's not. If you're tired and need a nap already, then it's time to go home. You can sleep the rest of the day inside. And I'll need to cut your meals down, as you must be more out of shape than I thought."

Mosey rolled over and struggled to his feet. His fat, squat body looked bulldoggish, matching the stubborn look on his face.

–Shoulda given me gravy for breakfast. It gives me energy.

"Like hell," she muttered, finally realizing she was outside and although people talked to their pets all the time, she didn't want to appear crazy to any passersby. At the crosswalk, she called the dogs to her side and made it across in one piece. Of course, it was a small town and traffic was light at this hour on a Saturday morning.

Once on the other side of the road, it was only a few minutes to her yard. She walked around the outside first. Thankfully, there were no broken windows, and as far as she could see, nothing had been disturbed. She didn't want to make an insurance claim. She could barely afford the premiums now.

Unlocking the door, she pushed it wide open and ushered the dogs inside. Once in, she took off the two leashes so the dogs wouldn't get tangled. Her house seemed impossibly full. Skirting the moving bodies and wagging tails, she checked out her living room – normal like everything else. She walked through the kitchen, only sorry the neighborhood intruder hadn't washed her dishes while she was gone. It was the least he could have done for disturbing her night's rest.

After a quick trip to her bathroom she doubled-checked her bedroom. Again, everything appeared normal. Sighing with relief, she realized how bothered she'd been. She navigated through the chaos of animals until she was back in her tiny kitchen.

She washed her dishes and enjoyed an hour in her own space, began a load of laundry, checked her messages and even called Jane. No answer. That figured. It was Saturday and Jane wouldn't be out of bed for hours yet.

Finally, with her chores done, she turned to survey the living room and had to laugh. Dogs lolled wherever they'd found space.

There was a large park about a block away. She could go down the alley and around the corner to avoid cars. The park would be perfect. No traffic, almost no people and a wide open space for the dogs to run.

–*Yes, let's do it.*

"Damn. I forgot you can read my mind."

–*Yes, and now I know. Park, park, park.* His chant turned to a half howl and before she knew it, the rest of the dogs were on their feet, staring at her standing there holding their leashes in her hand.

"Okay, fine," she shouted, "but we have to come back later and switch over the laundry."

Mosey headed to the back door.

—*Whatever. Park, park, park.*

***

The park was mostly empty, but then she wasn't walking on the normal pathways. She thought the dogs would prefer the wooded area along the side. As she enjoyed the stroll, she wondered about the many unanswered phone messages she'd left for her old shrink.

Somehow, the concept of a talking dog didn't bother her quite so much anymore.

Just then, Mosey stopped and threw her a jowly grin, making her roll her eyes. "I'm not saying that I like talking to you, because you don't actually talk. At least not out loud." She paused and wondered. "At least I don't think so. You're talking in my head, so maybe I'm making you up and maybe not. Either way, I'm the only person affected, so, I can choose how I respond to you."

—*If only you'd learn to talk back to me in your head when we're in public.*

She laughed. "Yeah, if only."

At the park, she unclipped the leashes and let the dogs roam. She wandered along the edge of the trees, enjoying the unusual experience. For the first time, she had to wonder if it really was bad to be talking with an imaginary friend – even if it were a dog. Sure, having more real friends would help, but in lieu of the real thing, was this so bad? Of course Mosey didn't quite fit the bill. He was real flesh and blood. Not imaginary. Still, telepathic dogs must come under the heading of 'imaginary.'

Maybe she should just give it a rest and accept what she was experiencing. If and when her shrink decided to respond to her messages, she could make a decision about seeing him or not. Besides, by then, maybe Mosey wouldn't be talking anymore.

A large grove of evergreen trees lay up ahead. She wandered over, looking for a place to sit. The dogs ran to her, then ran away again, delighted with their outdoor playtime. She wished she'd brought her camera. Her aunt would never believe she had been here walking all these dogs.

She sat down to rest for a minute, and glimpsed a bright blue item deeper in the shade. She stood up and walked closer. The color intrigued her. There was a familiar look to it. She had to work her way under the low-lying boughs to grab it. Crawling back out again, she straightened with it in her hand. Turning the square item over, she froze.

It was a picture frame from her house. Her name was written in the space where the picture went. She'd written it herself. The frame had held a photo taken last year when she'd celebrated the purchase of her first house.

The picture was missing. Even worse, she hadn't noticed that this picture had disappeared. When had she noticed it last? Yesterday morning. She was sure because she'd put her book down beside it.

So. Someone *had* broken into her house and stolen this. Her mind stalled on that idea.

Someone? It had to have been last night's intruder. Nothing else made sense.

Oh shit. The intruder might have her picture. That thought creeped her out. Holding the empty frame in her hand, she didn't dare contemplate what could happen if he returned –and she was home.

She swallowed hard. Her stomach revolted at the thought and she started to shake.

"Hey what's wrong?" An older couple stood off to one side, staring at her with concern. "Are you okay?"

Ninna tried hard to smile. "Yes, thank you. I'm suddenly not feeling well." She turned to look for the dogs. She needed to go back. Not home. Back to Stuart's. She needed to leave the park – now.

"Mosey, come on, boy. Let's go. Goober. Brie. It's time to go." She whistled hard. Giving the older couple an apologetic smile, she headed back the way they'd come, the dogs running to catch up. She didn't know why Mosey wasn't talking to her. Usually his sarcasm underlined everything she said or did. Today, right now, it seemed he was actually being considerate. Or maybe it was because there were other people around. Not likely, though. Clipping the leashes back on the other two dogs, she called the remaining ones into line and picked up the pace as her nerves started to get to her.

All she could think about was getting inside. Safe. She felt vulnerable outside.

She felt violated.

And didn't know what to do about it.

***

There she was. Troy stopped and stared.

While heading to the corner store for smokes, he'd cut across the park, taking the same route he'd taken the night before, only in reverse – and he'd almost missed her. The sun beamed high above him, making him squint.

Where'd the dogs come from? There'd been no sign of any pets in her house. And what was she holding in her other hand? The frame... *Damn.* He lost sight of her through the trees. In a panic, he ran to catch up.

He had to be cautious. She couldn't be allowed to see him. Too bad she'd found the frame. Another careless mistake. Her fault again. He frowned trying to figure it all out.

Maybe she'd been house-sitting for a neighbour. He patted his back pocket, where her picture was folded and tucked in his wallet. His mood lightened. What a perfect opportunity to find out what was going on.

Following at a safe distance behind, he watched as she went inside a huge house just across and slightly down the street from hers.

Interesting.

He'd have to check that out a little closer.

"How do you know it's yours?" Jane asked in her most reasonable tone. This time, she'd picked up two sub sandwiches and both girls sat in Stuart's kitchen for a late lunch. The dogs, ever eager to help, sprawled on the floor in a large circle, all eyes tracking the food as they ate. Even Tiny's miniature mouth opened every time Ninna opened hers. She didn't know if human food was good or bad for a kitten, but she couldn't imagine it would be ideal.

"I wrote the date and location inside the frame where the photo goes."

"It's kind of creepy."

"Kind of? It's way creepy." Ninna opened her mouth to take a bite as Tiny mimicked her with an open mouth of his own. Groaning, Ninna turned to face Jane, who appeared oblivious to all the animals' silent pleas. Jane had the shortest attention span of anyone she knew, and if issues didn't revolve around her, they were dropped into that vast space of 'not important.'

Ninna couldn't help grinning at her friend. Jane might be shallow, but she was loyal.

"So what are you going to do about it?"

"I don't know. I guess I need to call the police but I'm not sure it would help. Fill out a police report so it's on record, but then what?" Ninna shrugged. "I'm hoping that having gone through my place once, the person figured out I didn't have anything worth stealing and won't bother coming back."

She took another bite of her sandwich, and almost choked on the hot peppers. Jane loved everything super spicy.

"Or he's decided he likes the way you look and now wants to meet you in person – at night."

The heat of the peppers combined with her stomach acids and threatened to shoot the meal back up. Sourly, she said, "Thanks for that. As if I didn't have enough to worry about."

"It would be foolish not to consider it. Why else would he have kept the picture?"

"Maybe whoever it was tossed the picture first, thinking to keep the frame and then decided the frame wasn't worth keeping, either. Personally, I like the sound of that option much better than yours." She popped the last of her sandwich into her mouth and washed it down with a large drink of water.

–*Naive.*

Ninna stiffened. It was one thing for Mosey to talk, but it was another thing for him to have that kind of vocabulary.

"What I don't want you to do, is talk yourself down so much that you relax about the intruder. If he's a bad ass, then we have to do something to keep you safe. Surely, when Stuart comes back you could borrow...a dog." She motioned at the mess of canines lying on the floor, and added, "Just in case."

Ninna thought about that and her mood brightened. That was a great idea. "I hadn't considered that. I wonder how he'd feel about it?"

"These guys aren't his, right? So it would be the same as if you fostered the animal for the Center. You'd just be fostering one or two of *these* dogs."

–Me, pick me.

From the corner of her eye, she could see Mosey swinging his big head, his ears slapping up against his head. *How did he do that?*

"That lab is gentle, but I bet he's a great watchdog. Then that little white dog probably would never shut up. They'd be great together." Jane considered the animals around them, her gaze sharp and assessing.

Ninna had to admit the weekend had opened her eyes to the benefits of having a pet. She just didn't know if she was up to a full-time commitment. That was a responsibility she had yet to take on. Even her past relationships had stalled at the commitment point.

"Of course, it will also keep you nicely connected to Stuart. He looks like a nice man. A slow, steady kind of guy."

Slow? Stuart? Hell no. Especially not after the morning phone conversation. She had to admit staying connected to him sounded pretty damn good. She stayed silent while Jane continued on with her assessment of Stuart.

"He's going to take some time before he puts the moves on you. You want to be ready when he does."

Heat crept up Ninna's face. She got up to refill her water glass, trying to stop the blush from totally taking over her face. Jane would jump on her in an instant if she noticed.

"Of course, if you aren't interested, let me know. Because I just might have to mine that ground myself."

Ninna spun around to stare at her friend. Jane could sometimes be so dense as to be unbelievable.

"Ha, gotcha!" Jane jumped up, triumphant. The flush returned tenfold. "Oh, you."

"Do you really think I didn't notice how interested you are? Girl, credit me with some smarts. That's the only reason I stayed after you left that first night. I wanted to check out what he was like. Make sure he was good enough for you."

Ninna stared at her over her glass of water. "Really?"

"Really." She grinned. "Admit it. You thought I was putting the moves on him, didn't you?"

Ninna stepped over the lab and flopped back on her kitchen chair. "Yeah, kinda."

"Look, if and when I put the moves on a guy, that guy gets moved my way, if you know what I mean. No, I wanted to make sure he was decent. You've had a rough year. You need to have someone put some fun back in your life. You need to live a little. Now this Stuart, he's got a nice bit of cash, he's decent, single and he looks after his own." She motioned at Tiny, still huddled on the table. "You can always tell what a guy is like by checking out how he cares for his animals."

"He does look after them, doesn't he?" Surveying the spotless kitchen, Ninna realized the animals hadn't made much of a mess. What had she been worried about?

"So when will he be back?"

"Maybe tonight. He wasn't sure when he called this morning."

"Cool. Stay here and you'll be at the right place at the right time." Jane waggled her eyebrows in a way that always made Ninna laugh.

"We're hardly to that stage."

"Honey, you can jump into that stage any time. And it moves everything else forward at top speed."

Ninna shook her head. "So not happening. I probably will sleep here, because Stuart might *not* come back tonight. I'd worry about the animals."

"Whatever reason you tell yourself, is fine with me." Jane smirked, snatched up the paper wrappings from the subs and tossed them into the garbage. "Dishes done. So now what?"

"No idea. You?"

"Let's do a girl's afternoon and go to the mall?"

Ninna groaned. "You and your shopping trips. I don't have any money to shop with, remember?"

"You're working now, remember?" Jane sauntered into the living room. "First, though, I'm going to explore." She ran upstairs, with several of the dogs scrambling to keep up with her.

Ninna contemplated following, then decided against it. Jane didn't need any encouragement. Instead, Ninna busied herself washing the animals' food dishes and wiping up the table and counters.

A scream ripped through the house.

Jane flew down the hallway toward Ninna, her face white, her hands flapping in front of her. "Oh, my God, he's got a snake. There's a damn snake in the house."

Ninna grinned, started to laugh, then bent over howling. "You should see your face. It serves you right for snooping. Yes, he's got a snake, but thankfully, the snake has been fed, so I don't have to do the honors. But if you'd like you cou—"

Jane's gaze widened with horror. "Feed it? Oh, gross!"

"Yeah, I told him I wasn't having anything to do with this zoo if it meant dropping a live mouse in there."

Jane's face paled even further. "Live mouse? Oh, my God. Isn't there a law against that?"

"I doubt it. Snakes are entitled to live too, you know."

Jane reared back and stared at her. "Is this *you* speaking?" She shook her head. "There's no way in hell a snake should be given life at the cost of a little mouse."

Ninna laughed. "I'm not going to argue that point."

A loud roar of a vehicle sounded. The dogs went crazy. Ninna raised her eyebrows and walked over to the front window. "It's not Stuart." As she approached the front door, it opened in front of her. The dogs swarmed the stranger, overwhelming him with their joy.

A tall broad-shouldered man walked in and stopped when he caught sight of the two women. "Uhm, hi?"

"Hi back." Ninna studied the red hair and lanky build and remembered what Stuart had said. "I don't suppose you're Stuart's brother, by any chance?"

His grin flashed sheer devilment across the room. Ninna blinked. Jane shifted into action. She slid closer. "Hi, I'm Jane."

Male appreciation lit the deep blue eyes. "Hi. I'm Ian. Stuart is my older brother."

Jane lit up brighter, if that were possible. Such information was gold to her ears. Ninna stepped forward. "I'm Ninna. I don't know if Stuart told you, but I'm looking after the animals while he's gone."

Surprise washed over his face. "Then I didn't need to rush over here. We've been playing phone tag all week. I was supposed to look after these guys, but wasn't sure I could make it to town in time. He mentioned that he had lined up someone to help out but that they might not sleep over, so I stopped in to check."

Walking to the big bay window, Ninna pointed out her small house. "I live just across the street, so it seemed like an easy solution."

"And I live just a couple of blocks away." Jane stepped between them. "Are you a vet, too?"

Ian laughed. "Not likely. I'm in construction. I like these animals just fine, but there's no way I could deal with all the hurt and dying ones." He reached down to greet each dog. "These dogs are special. They've all got a story of some kind to tell."

"In construction?" Jane wouldn't be sidetracked. She was also busy feasting her eyes on him.

Ninna had to laugh at her friend. "I understand from Stuart that you're building a house for him on an acreage close by?"

Ian grinned. "Yes." He walked down the hallway, spied Tiny on the table and snagged him up for a big hug. "These guys are going to love the new place. Over ten acres, fenced, with a big yard, runs, and a huge space that will eventually become a place where Stuart can look after the injured animals. The yard is designed to maximize the space for Stuart's never-ending stream of 'pets in need,' as he calls them. We both own the lot beside his house, so if need be, we can expand."

"Wow." Jane said it softly, her admiration obvious. Ninna watched her friend with raised brow. Jane didn't seem to be acting this time. Interesting. Maybe her friend had hidden depths after all.

"He's got some plans." Ninna wasn't sure it was sensible to build with the idea to expand later. Why not just build what you need in the first place? Then again, the budget might only go so far.

—It's got nothing to do with money. Stuart's loaded.

Ninna almost answered but caught herself at the last moment. She shot a glare at Mosey, hoping he'd shut up again.

—Not likely. Can't wait to get to the new house. Then we can spend more time outside. It's time for another walk, you know.

"So, does this mean I'm off the hook?" Ninna couldn't quell the sense of disappointment. She'd been looking forward to seeing Stuart and maybe having a quiet evening with him. Ian looked like a lot of fun, but he was almost too energetic for her taste.

"No way. If you're here, then I'm free to go to town and enjoy myself."

Jane laughed. "Wow, that sounds like fun. It is Saturday, after all."

"It is, and I have tickets to tonight's concert. Wasn't sure I'd be able to make it. Now, however, I can go." He grinned. "Can't say thanks enough to you for staying here. I have a place to crash in town, so no need to worry."

Jane's shoulders deflated.

"I have two tickets, if someone wants to come along…" He stared directly at Jane, easily cutting Ninna out of that loop.

Ninna hadn't expected the relief she felt not to be included. Jane, on the other hand, lit up like a sparkler and said, "I do. We can leave Ninna here to look after the animals."

Ninna rolled her eyes. "Sure, leave the babysitter home, while the children go off and play."

Jane was immediately contrite. "I'm sorry. You don't really mind, do you? I know you're a little freaked over that whole intruder thing, but you'll be safe here with the dogs."

"Intruder?" Ian frowned, walking over to the fridge and pouring himself a glass of milk. "Stuart mentioned something about a mess of break-ins."

"I called the cops last night."

"And..." Jane filled him in on the picture frame.

Ian leaned back against the sink, his arms folded across his chest. "I definitely don't like the sound of that. Please stay here until Stuart gets home. Talk to the police about the picture frame you found and maybe talk to Stuart about a watchdog. I'm not sure you should be alone after that, either."

"What am I supposed to do over the long term? That's my home. I can't stay away." Ninna tried to sound reasonable. She wasn't like Ian and Stuart. She didn't have hefty bank accounts to stay somewhere else until this guy was caught.

"Can you beef up your security system? A good system is a great deterrent." He filled his glass with water and left it in the sink. "Obviously, whatever you have right now isn't enough. It also worries me that this guy entered and left, yet you didn't know. What's the chance he's done it before?"

Shivers raced down her spine. "I have no idea. I don't even want to think about that possibility."

"But you said yourself, there'd been a couple of evenings when you wondered if someone was outside. Maybe someone is stalking you. A Peeping Tom?"

"Okay, now you're scaring me. That's not helping, you know. I can't just stay with Stuart all the time."

"Still, you might consider that option for the time being. Stuart wouldn't mind. And there's lots of room here. " Ian checked his watch. "The concert starts in a couple of hours. I could use a meal before then." He lifted his head, eyed Jane up and down once, and added, "I suppose you want to change?"

Jane widened her eyes. "Hell, yeah. I have wheels parked at Ninna's place, too."

"Why don't I follow you to your place and we'll drive from there. You can change, then we'll head out for dinner and the concert."

The two walked to the front door, so into each other and how to handle the logistics of two sets of wheels, they barely said good-bye to Ninna. Within moments, Ian had backed down the driveway and driven off with her best friend.

He was like a heavy north wind. Blew in, picked up what he wanted and blew right back out again. A perfect match for Jane.

Ninna, on the other hand, saw herself as more like a warm summer breeze. She wafted in, checked things out and wafted back and around again. Stuart was more like her. At least she hoped he was.

The phone rang while she served up dinner for the dogs. It must cost him a fortune to feed this many animals. She checked the caller ID and picked up.

"Hi, Stuart."

"Hey, how's the day been, and where are you? Your place or mine?" Instantly, that suggestive phrase went through her. For all his brother's debonair devil-may-care, let's-live-while-we're-young attitude that had caught Jane's interest, it had left Ninna cold. Stuart, on the other hand, was making her insides melt.

"I'm at your place. Your brother just blew in on his own and blew out again with my friend Jane on his arm."

A shocked moment was followed by a bellow of laughter. "That's a perfect description of him. Jane's just his style."

Ninna walked to the living room and curled up on the couch to visit. "True enough. Where are you?"

"At the airport. With any luck, I'll be home tonight. I'm not counting on it yet, not until the plane actually takes off."

Excitement bounced around her insides. She'd see him tonight. "And if all goes well, what time do you think you'll get here?"

"A couple of hours – three at the most." His voice sharpened. "And, no, I don't want you feeling like you're not needed there in the meantime."

She had to laugh. "How'd you know I was thinking that?"

"I think I have a good idea of who you are inside. I'm hoping to see you tonight. They're calling passengers for my flight. I have to go." He hung up. Ninna stared at the phone in her hand. Happy butterflies danced in her stomach.

–Oh, brother. Are you going to moon around after him now? It's walk time, you know.

Even the nudge from Mosey didn't distract her from the joy welling in her heart. She might actually have met someone who liked her as much as she liked him. Wouldn't that be a nice change? Checking out the food dishes, she realized all had been emptied already. The lab was apparently happy to lick the last bits from each bowl. She'd take them back to the park, on the other side this time. Maybe even pick up a coffee... And if a baseball game was happening, she'd sit outside for an hour or so. She snagged up the leashes and the dogs came running.

She could get used to this.

Chapter 6

Ninna fell asleep on the couch around ten, with the TV still on and the dogs at her feet. She hadn't intended to do that. Something woke her. She lay still for a moment, trying to reorient herself. As the dogs never moved, she decided the noise was on the street. She stretched out and contemplated making the shift to her bed upstairs. She had to smile. Tiny had moved to curl up on the back of the couch. He looked so cute.

Knowing there couldn't be anything wrong if the dogs were so unconcerned, she decided to stay where she was a little longer. The dogs got up and sniffed the doors and wandered around the house. They didn't bark, but they did rumble. Just not very hard or for very long. However, as she'd only spent one night here, she wasn't sure what normal behavior was for them.

She got up and checked out the window. As far as she could see, there was nothing outside. The dogs continued sniffing. When they were near the garage door, the lab and the boxer, started growling, deep harsh sounds that scared her almost as much as the possible reason for them. She pressed her ear against the door but still couldn't hear anything. Mosey curled his lip and a deep growl ripped out of his throat. Ninna checked that the door was locked before returning to the kitchen. She closed the drapes and stayed away from the window just in case someone was watching.

Where was Stuart? He'd thought he'd be back by now. She wanted him to return, and soon. She hated this. She ran to check the locks and set the security system – something she'd set hours ago. With her heart pounding, she whipped through the various checks and only after the last one did she breathe a sigh of relief. Turning away from the security panel, she realized every dog and cat had followed her on her journey. Now they sat, not a growl or curled lip among them, just patiently staring up at her. What were they waiting for? *Oh, yes...*

"Last trip outside, then bed." They all looked up at her, innocence on their faces. She turned off the alarm on the back door, and let them out.

The backyard was in virtual blackness. She found the light on the inside wall and clicked on a large spotlight that lit up the bulk of the yard. The dogs welcomed the chance to sniff around, and scattered to find their favourite patches and a last chance to lift a leg. Not one growled or barked. She relaxed slightly until she realized there was no sign of Mosey.

"Mosey? Where are you? Damn, I don't need this." She was standing on the deck, with her back to the kitchen when she heard him.

Sniff.

—Like I do. Not telling me we're going out like that is just mean. You owe me. A second dinner should take care of it.

Relieved, she spun around and glowered at him. "Ha, fat chance. Where were you, anyway?" She watched as he waddled through the doorway like he owned the place. "You're supposed to be on a diet, remember?" She gave the dogs a couple more minutes, then called them back inside, did a head count and locked the door up tight. Then she made sure she reset the alarm.

—Dinner?

"You had dinner." She refused to give in.

She wanted a hot bath. That would make her feel better and help pass the time…although she didn't want to be soaking in the bath when Stuart arrived. That would be a little too suggestive.

With the dogs calm, she headed to the Jacuzzi to relax. She'd hear Stuart well before he made it upstairs, surely.

She ran the warm water into the huge tub. She thought she heard the dogs barking, but when she went out into the hallway to check, they had quieted again. Crazy.

Back in the bathroom, she added bath salts from a jar sitting off to one side. The scent of lavender filled the room. Inhaling appreciatively, she undressed and slipped into the warm water. "Oh, what a slice of heaven," she whispered to the empty room. She couldn't help loving the decadence of this house. Compared to her tiny nest, this was ultimate luxury.

Wallowing in the warmth, she could feel the tension and stress slip off her shoulders and wash away in the water. Sleep beckoned so strongly she almost drifted off.

It was only as the water cooled she realized how much time had passed. Pulling the plug, she struggled to get out of the water, feeling more tired than she could believe. Her limbs were heavy as lead. There was a spare robe hanging on the back of the door. She wrapped herself up in it and used the second towel to wrap around her head.

As she went to open the door, she heard it.

Something heavy moved beyond her bedroom. Too big to be the dogs. Stuart? No, he'd have called out to her. What could it be? Uncertain, she stood still and silent. Damn, this would be a good time for Mosey to hear her thoughts.

–Mosey?

There was almost an answer. Mentally, she called him again, getting a somewhat fuzzy response. She didn't understand it. Fear slammed into her. Something was wrong. *But what?* She stared at the closed bathroom door in horror. Then she heard a sound that made her blood freeze. A door closed.

Her bedroom door. Oh, shit.

She was stuck in a bathroom wearing nothing but a robe, while something she wasn't going to like waited for her in the bedroom. Her clothes, where the hell where they? Dumped in a pile at the door. She got dressed as quietly and as quickly as possible, her mind frantically sorting through her options. She searched for her cell phone. Yes, it was in her pants pocket. She quickly texted

Stuart, telling him something was wrong. Then she texted Jane.

Turning her phone to vibrate, she waited for a response. She kept her fright in check, just barely as her gaze zeroed in on the door. *Shit. It wasn't locked.* How could she lock it and not have someone on the other side hear? She had no choice. She reached up and turned the bolt.

Snick.

She held her breath. Then released it. So far so good. Now what could she find in a bathroom to use as a weapon? She stared around the small room, her panic building. The only window was too high up to reach. There were no aerosol sprays. Outside of a skin loofah – like that was going to help – she couldn't see anything of value. The towel, but what could she do with it? She was no martial arts expert. She'd often thought of doing some self-defence courses, but hadn't gotten that far…unfortunately. Now she desperately wished she had.

Her phone vibrated in her hand. She quickly read the text. Stuart. He was only blocks away, and he'd contacted the police. She read his text: 'Stay hidden. I'll be there in a few minutes.'

"Oh, thank God." Keeping her head down, she sat down, her back pressed against the door. Whoever was on the other side had to know she was here. There was no other place for her to be. The draining bathwater had probably alerted him. *Shit.*

–Ninna? Where are you?

She straightened. *Mosey! Thank heavens. I'm in the bathroom. Who's in the bedroom?*

–I don't know. I just woke up. I'll come upstairs and see.

Ninna winced, wanting to scream out for help. *No, I don't want you to get hurt. Stuart's on his way.*

–Good. Almost there. Uh oh.

She spun around on her bum to stare helplessly at the closed door, wishing she knew who was on the other side. *Uh oh? Uh oh, what? Who's there?*

–I don't know him. He doesn't look dog friendly. He looks mean.

Oh, shit. *Get out of the way. Don't let him see you. He might hurt you. Where are the other dogs? Why aren't they with you?* She didn't want anything to happen to him or the other animals.

–I'm not going to get hurt. Still, this is not a nice man. The dogs are sleeping downstairs in the

front room. He sprayed us with something. Stay in there. Uh oh!

What? Mosey, what? Her breath caught. She closed her eyes as fear stole her breath.

–He's coming to the bathroom door.

Oh, shit. Ninna shuffled her bum to the door. With her breath caught in her throat, she waited.

"Ninna? Is that you?"

The guy in the bedroom, a voice she didn't recognize, called her by name. Horrified, she stared into the full-length mirror on the opposite wall. She didn't recognize *his* voice. But he knew *her* name.

The male voice, lighter, younger than Stuart's, spoke again. "Ninna. Sorry, didn't mean to surprise you. Come on out and let's talk."

Talk? Was he nuts? There's no way she was going out there.

"I've been admiring you from a distance for weeks now. Saw you by accident when I walked past your little house. You're gorgeous, you know that?" He paused. "I just want to get to know you better."

She barely held a small scream from breaking free. Silence was her best bet. She hugged her knees, rocking back and forth. She stuffed a corner of the towel into her mouth to keep the small panicked squeals from coming out. Texting didn't work with her hands shaking so bad. She was almost paralyzed by her terror.

Stuart...someone, please hurry!

"Ninna, come on out. You don't have to be scared of me. I just want to talk to you."

How the hell had he gotten into the damn house? As if he could read her mind, he answered the question himself.

"When you came back after letting the dogs out the last time, I crept in through the garage. Got a great spray a friend of mine made up. Put the dogs out quick. Don't worry though, it won't hurt them none. Came straight upstairs and went into the master, expecting to find you there. It made me feel good to know you weren't sharing his bed. You were waiting for me, weren't you?" His voice became louder and she could barely hear his footsteps but sensed he walked right up to the door. Her heart pounded so heavily it was hard to hear his next words. She strained to hear.

"You should have stayed home. That little house is perfect for you. For us."

Her eyes widened. *Oh God, Mosey. He's crazy.*

—Yeah, he doesn't look too good. He's got a mess of ropes and things in his hands, too.

Oh, God. Oh, God. Stuart, where are you? Please let the police get here soon. How long could it take to drive a few blocks? Ropes. Oh, God. Mosey, you stay away from him. He'll hurt you. You can't run that fast.

Mosey sniffled, but it sounded too close to a real snicker for her peace of mind.

—Oh ye of little faith. You never did believe in me.

I mean it. As much as I may not have had anything to do with pets before this last week, I have to admit that you've all grown on me. I don't want anything bad to happen to any of you.

Just then the doorknob above her head turned. She swallowed hard.

The lock held – but for how long?

"Ninna. Come on out. I don't like this door between us. I don't want to break the door down, but I will if I have to."

Any decent-sized male could break down the puny door in a few minutes. She stared at it in dread.

"I just want to visit for awhile."

Like hell. If that was the case, there was no reason to have brought ropes.

Just then sirens approached. Her heart jumped. God, please let the police be coming to help her.

"Did you call the cops, you bitch? You know you've been teasing me all this time. Inviting me in. This is your fault. What a fucking bitch. Don't worry, you'll get yours."

He kicked the bathroom door hard. She shuddered as the wood rippled against her back from the force. She could hear him running toward her, then smash, he hit the door again. The lock almost gave way. With the next try, it probably would. What could she do?

–Stay quiet.

Mosey?

"What the fuck was that?"

The voice yelled right on the other side of the door. She freaked out.

Mosey, what are you doing?

Screams from the bedroom had her jumping to her feet. She cried out, "Mosey, stop, you're going to get hurt."

"Get it off me! Get it off meeeeee!"

Then all hell broke loose.

Barks, howls, yips added to the yells and roars that filled the bedroom and more sirens filled the night. Ninna huddled lower to the floor and waited, whimpers caught deep in her throat as sounds of chaos washed over her.

Then everything went silent.

A tentative voice called out, "Ninna? It's Stuart. It's okay, you can come out now. We've got him."

She closed her eyes in relief. "Stuart?"

"Yes, it's me. Unlock the door. It's safe now." Then Mosey's voice filled her mind.

—It's good ole Stuart. That bad guy isn't walking so good anymore. I bit him in the ass. Blech.

"Oh my God." Ninna was half laughing and half crying by the time she had the door unlocked. Opening it, she collapsed into Stuart's arms. He held her close. "Shhhh, it's all right now. Everything's going to be fine." A few long moments later, he drew back slightly. "The police are here. I think they're going to need to talk to you. "

She sniffled but let him lead her over to where several officers stood. Wiping her eyes on her sleeve, she smiled tremulously at the female deputy. "Thank you so much for coming to my rescue."

"We've been after this guy for a long time. We were afraid his behavior would escalate. We're just happy we caught him before he did anything worse. If you feel up to it, we need to take your statement." The deputy led her downstairs and into the kitchen.

There, with a cup of bracing tea, and the dogs milling about in the excitement, Ninna told them what she knew. From the break-ins to finding the picture frame to tonight's frightening experience, she tried to give a coherent retelling of events. Stuart stood behind her, one hand on her shoulder for support.

She withheld the Mosey information. They'd just think she was crazy.

Speaking of Mosey, where was he? He deserved a big hug and a huge bowl of gravy. She glanced around, but with all the cops and the animals, she couldn't see him. She turned her attention back to the deputy. "Where's the intruder? Please, may I see him? I'd like to have a real face to put on that monster."

Stuart started to protest, but she cut him off. "No, it will help. Better to have a face, than a thousand imaginary ones to haunt me."

The deputy left for a moment then came back, a laptop in her hand. She brought up a picture. "This is a good likeness. He's got a long rap sheet, including sexual assault."

Swallowing heavily at the last words, Ninna took a look at the man. He was a stranger. She didn't think she'd ever seen him before. "How is it that he's been stalking me, yet I've never caught sight of him anywhere?"

The deputy sighed as if she'd observed too much in life and nothing surprised her anymore. "Unfortunately, that's all too common."

Stuart squeezed her shoulder gently. "Where is he now?"

"He's been taken to the hospital to have that bite looked after, then he'll spend the next few years in jail, if not longer this time, thanks to you." The deputy closed the laptop and stood up. "Try to get some rest. Be sure to consider getting professional help if you find you're having trouble dealing with tonight's events."

With a quick smile, Ninna said, "I will, and thank you."

Ninna stood and walked to the front door, Stuart at her side, his arm firmly wrapped around her shoulders as everyone prepared to leave. Glancing at the clock, she realized it was three in the morning. They stood on the doorstep until the vehicles pulled away.

As they walked back inside, she said, "So much for coming home early and getting some sleep. You might have been better off staying at the conference."

He pulled her into a warm, comforting embrace. "Don't ever say that. I'm so glad I made it here in time and wish I'd been hours earlier."

Pulling back slightly so she could see his face, she said, "Maybe. But at least this way the guy is caught and I can stop looking over my shoulder."

Keeping an arm around her, Stuart locked up the front door and reset the alarms. "I can't believe he was so slick as to get past the dogs, then come after you...well that's more than scary..."

He turned off the rest of the lights, and then led her to the stairs. "Although, if the dogs were sprayed, and weren't in your room until the end, and you were locked in the bathroom, how'd he get bitten? He was screaming to get the dog off him, but in the chaos, I never did see which one he was screaming about."

Ninna laughed. "That was Mosey. He bit him on the butt. I owe him a big thank you for that."

Stuart gave her an odd look as they arrived at the spare room. He opened the door and stopped at the entrance. Frowning, he turned back to her. "Why don't you sleep in my room tonight and I'll sleep here? This isn't a good place for you to be tonight."

She grimaced as she looked around. "No, you're also tired. Besides, if I let the dogs sleep in here with me, then I won't be scared. I'm more shook up now that it's over."

Walking around the room, she realized she wasn't afraid. "You know something. I will sleep here. Mosey is sure to join me, as will at least one of the other dogs. I'm so tired that I'm sure I'll be fine."

At his lack of response, she looked at him curiously.

"You appear to more comfortable around the dogs now. Is there one that you fell for the most?"

She laughed. "Caught me out, did you? Well, to be honest, I found all of them to be friendly.

But I did, against my better judgement, fall for that oversized basset hound."

An odd light came into his eyes, a tender smile whispered across his lips. "Really? Mosey, huh? Come here for a second, I have something to show you."

He led the way to his bedroom with all the dogs traipsing behind. Opening the door wide, he turned on the overhead light and pointed out a big painting on the far wall. "See that?"

She walked closer and chuckled, shooting him a big grin. "That dog's ego is already huge, why would you make it bigger by giving him a full-size portrait?"

"Go closer."

She walked right up to it, loving the amazing detail. "The artist even got that look in his eye. This is perfect. Who painted it?"

"My mother. She was an incredible artist. She passed away about seventeen years ago now."

Silence filled the room as she digested what he said. She frowned. "He doesn't look that old." She laughed. "Oh, I get it. The painting was of his sire?"

Stuart, with a gentle look on his face, said, "No, it isn't. Look at the plaque underneath."

Shooting him a confused look, Ninna leaned closer and read aloud, "Mosey, beloved friend to the Macintosh family. 1979-1994."

She spun around, confusion on her face, but inside shock, a dawning horror, and an inkling of understanding filtered in. Leaning against Stuart's leg, Mosey sat in his half-slouched position, his jowls hanging much the way she'd first seen him at the Center – laughing at her.

"Am I crazy?" She took a deep breath and added, "He's slouched at your left side."

Stuart smiled, a touch of melancholy on his face as he looked down. "He was my dog, you know. I've always wanted to see him, but since his death, only a few special people have had the privilege."

She swallowed hard. Yes, she'd finally connected the dots, but this was no time for assumptions. Not when she'd gone through years of therapy and medications for something similar. Had everyone been wrong?

"Death?"

"Yes. You've been seeing Mosey's ghost, my dear. And if you're really lucky, he's been talking to you." At the stunned guilty look on her face, he laughed, "He has been, hasn't he? Apparently he has a colorful turn of phrase."

Ninna could only nod as she tried to process the information. She didn't have an overactive imagination. She wasn't crazy. *Maybe she'd never been crazy?* Mosey had existed and apparently, according to more people than just her, he still did. A funny sound escaped.

With a big grin, Stuart said, "How perfect that you, who've never had anything to do with animals and was scared to look after a couple of them, have been honored by the presence of my beloved old pet and best friend."

Ninna's stunned gaze went from Mosey, to Stuart and back to Mosey.

Mosey opened that huge jowly mouth and spoke as loudly as she'd been speaking to Stuart – as clear as a bell.

–Boo, now I see you – and finally, you see me!

Then he re-formed those crazy skin folds and flashed that huge grin at her.

–Gravy?

Other Books from Dale Mayer

Dangerous Designs - a YA/Adult urban fantasy

Drawing is her world...but when her new pencil comes alive, it's his world too.

Her... Storey Dalton is seventeen and now boyfriendless after being dumped via Facebook. Drawing is her escape. It's like as soon as she gets down one image, a dozen more are pressing in on her. Then she realizes her pictures are almost drawing themselves...or is it that her new pencil is alive?

Him... Eric Jordan is a new Ranger and the only son of the Councilman to his world. He's crossed the veil between dimensions to retrieve a lost stylus. But Storey is already experimenting with her new pencil and what her drawings can do - like open portals.

It... The stylus is a soul-bound intelligence from Eric's dimension on Earth and uses Storey's unsuspecting mind to seek its way home, giving her an unbelievable power. She unwittingly opens a third dimension, one that held a dangerous predatory species banished from Eric's world centuries ago, releasing these animals into both dimensions.

Them... Once in Eric's homeland, Storey is blamed for the calamity sentenced to death. When she escapes, Eric is ordered to bring her back or face that same death penalty. With nothing to lose, can they work together across dimensions to save both their worlds?

Vampire in Denial - a YA/Adult paranormal fantasy

Blood doesn't just make her who she is...it also makes her what she is.

Like being a sixteen-year-old vampire isn't hard enough, Tessa's throwback human genes make her an outcast among her relatives. But try as she might, she can't get a handle on the vampire lifestyle and all the...blood.

Turning her back on the vamp world, she embraces the human teenage lifestyle—high school, peer pressure and finding a boyfriend. Jared manages to stir something in her blood. He's smart and fun and oh, so cute.

But Tessa's dream of a having the perfect boyfriend turns into a nightmare when vampires attack the movie theatre and kidnap her date .

Once again, Tessa finds herself torn between the human world and the vampire one. Will blood own out? Can she make peace with who she is as well as what?

Tuesday's Child - a romantic suspense with paranormal elements

What she doesn't want...is exactly what he needs.

Shunned and ridiculed all her life for something she can't control, Samantha Blair hides her psychic abilities and lives on the fringes of society. Against her will, however, she's tapped into a killer - or rather, his victims. Each woman's murder, blow-by-blow, ravages her mind until their death releases her back to her body. Sam knows she must go to the authorities, but will the rugged, no-nonsense detective in charge of tracking down the killer believe her?

Detective Brandt Sutherland only trusts hard evidence, yet Sam's visions offer clues he needs to catch a killer. The more he learns about her incredible abilities, however, the clearer it becomes that Sam's visions have put her in the killer's line of fire. Now Brandt must save her from something he cannot see or understand...and risk losing his heart in the process.

As danger and desire collide, passion raises the stakes in a game Sam and Brandt don't dare lose.

About the author:

Dale Mayer is a prolific multi-published writer. She's best known for her Psychic Visions series. Besides her romantic suspense/thrillers, Dale also writes paranormal romance and crossover young adult books in several different genres. To go with her fiction, she also writes nonfiction in many different fields with books available on resume writing, companion gardening and the US mortgage system. All her books are available in digital and print formats.

Published Young Adult books include:

Family Blood Ties Series
Vampire in Denial
Vampire in Distress
Vampire in Design
Vampire in Deceit
Vampire in Defiance

Design Series
Dangerous Designs
Deadly Designs
Darkest Designs

Standalone
In Cassie's Corner
Gem Stone Mystery

Published Adult Books:

Psychic Vision Series:
Tuesday's Child
Hide'n Go Seek,
Maddy's Floor
Garden of Sorrow
Knock, Knock...
Rare Find (April 2014)

By Death Series:
Touched by Death
Haunted by Death

Second Chances...at Love
Second Chances

Standalone
It's a Dog's Life - novella
Riana's Revenge – fantasy short story
Sian's Solution – a Family Blood Ties story

Connect with Dale Mayer Online:
Dale's Website – www.dalemayer.com
Twitter – http://twitter.com/#!/DaleMayer
Facebook –
http://www.facebook.com/DaleMayer.author

Made in the USA
Coppell, TX
18 July 2021

59086380R00085